Nick Saint
and the
Dasher of
Dreams

Jonathan Morris

ISBN 978-1-63784-543-1 (paperback)
ISBN 978-1-63784-544-8 (digital)

Copyright © 2024 by Jonathan Morris

All rights reserved. No part of this publication may be reproduced, distributed, or transmitted in any form or by any means, including photocopying, recording, or other electronic or mechanical methods without the prior written permission of the publisher. For permission requests, solicit the publisher via the address below.

Hawes & Jenkins Publishing
16427 N Scottsdale Road Suite 410
Scottsdale, AZ 85254
www.hawesjenkins.com

Printed in the United States of America

Chapter 1

It was Wednesday. Nick liked Wednesdays. Most people would feel that Wednesday was the tipping point of the week, the point where the end was in sight—not Nick. Nick believed that Wednesday was the real beginning of the week. That was the day he could pick up the paper and read actual news. The Monday paper had little to report, as little interesting business would occur on most weekends apart from the excess indulgences of the Monday to Friday working class while the affairs of the markets and governments were on hold. By Tuesday, there was still little to report, save for the usually dull Monday affairs. Nick wasn't certain, but he doubted he could remember a single Monday that was interesting. Wednesday, however, the news would finally have something to report. He could pick up his paper and get real news, or, to be precise, he could pick up his papers. Nick read no less than three every day, even on dull days. Typically, he would stop at the corner newsstand and get a paper of local, regional, and national circulation.

Nick still preferred a hard copy paper though he found them increasingly difficult to find. He was no Luddite and could pick up new technology faster than his aged visage would imply. Still, there was something about the feel and smell of a real paper that Nick enjoyed. He liked the sound it made as he turned and folded a page. He liked that he didn't get lost in clickbait and ads that obscured the story. He liked that the ads, by and large, were contained to Sunday and were easy to dispose of.

And that was how Nick was to be found on the first Wednesday of November. He had just finished reading *The Times* and was considering the possibility of an early lunch and a drink at his favorite pub, Paddy's, a short walk down the street from his office, when he heard the unmistakable sound of women's heels coming up the stairs. The buzzer rang from the intercom on his desk. Nick pushed the newspapers to one side of his desk and pulled a legal pad and pen from his drawer. The buzzer sounded a second time, and Nick unlocked the door as he said, "Come in," into the intercom. He heard the door swing open and the heels click down the hall toward his office.

The office door opened and in walked a thin, severe-looking woman. Nick guessed she was forty, maybe forty-five years old. She had sharp, high cheekbones and a long, thin nose, with exceptionally light-blue eyes, almost gray. She wore little makeup and maintained a very natural look. Her dirty blonde hair was pulled back into a tight bun without a single hair out of place. She wore short black heels and a black pantsuit with a plain white blouse underneath. Her jewelry was simple—a gold necklace, small-stone earrings, and a wedding band with a small princess-cut diamond.

Nick rose and took her coat. "Please, sit," he said, motioning to the only chair in the room besides his own.

She sat as he turned to hang her coat next to his. Looking around the office, she noted the old heavy drapes, forest green with gold filigree, hanging above the single-pane windows. The office was clean, well-kept, and plain. A small bookcase was on the wall to her right. Several old leather-bound volumes took up the lower shelves. The upper shelf had an assortment of knickknacks, a set of silver bells, an old oil lantern, and a simple clay pipe. She did not detect any hint of smoke in the room, however, and concluded the pipe had not been used in some time. A small space heater was running, taking the morning chill from the room. An old unused fireplace was behind Nick's desk. Holly wasn't sure, but she did not think she saw any chimneys in this otherwise nondescript four-story office building.

Nick sat down after hanging his guest's coat. He took a deep breath, folded his arms in front of his chest, and began. "I'm Nick Saint. I'm sure you already knew that. And you are?"

"I'm Holly Dash. I came here hoping you could help me. I'm looking for someone, and I'm hoping you can find him." She paused and then took a breath before adding, "But I'm sure you already knew that." She nodded toward a stack of newspapers on Nick's desk. Folded on top of the stack was the front-page news.

"So you're that Holly Dash. I see," Nick said.

Nick glanced at the paper. The top story in the local gazette featured the indictment of Stephen Dash, accused of embezzling millions from a children's charity. The Dasher of Dreams, they had called him. He was being held without bail as a flight risk. His supposed accomplice was still at large, as was the missing money, reportedly safely set away in an offshore account.

Nick continued, "And who is it you wish me to find?"

"I was told you were sharp, Nick. You've seen the papers. Who do you think I'm looking for?" Holly replied.

"A good lawyer, perhaps?" Nick offered. Nick was, in fact, fairly certain who Holly wanted to find, but Nick had found it was always good to be explicit when dealing with a client.

"I'm looking for the missing accountant," she replied. "Morgan Wood, CPA."

Morgan Wood, CPA, was the missing and supposed accomplice of Stephen Dash. From the papers, Nick knew that Wood had disappeared shortly before an audit was performed on the charity for which he worked and Stephen Dash was a board member and treasurer. Wood either was terrible at his job and had not noticed the missing cash or he was involved in its disappearance. To the former, he was a summa cum laude graduate in one of the top accounting programs in the country. He was the youngest partner in history at the prestigious firm Steale and Hyde. For some reason though, he gave up a big paycheck and went to work full-time for a children's charity at the age of forty-three. That part bothered Nick. Wood had money, power, and influence. Why give that up to work for a charity only to steal money he could have legally obtained?

"Aren't the police looking for him already? Why do you need me?"

Holly's face, a picture in stone, momentarily softened. Her eyes showed the faintest hint of moisture, her chin quivered, before resetting into a scowl. "You think the police are actually looking for him?"

"Why wouldn't they be? He's an accomplice in a multimillion-dollar theft. He's still at large and"—Nick tapped the paper on his desk—"it says they are, right here."

Holly's face reddened as she continued, "They aren't looking for him because they are using him as leverage against my husband. As long as he's free, they can offer a plea deal to Stephen: turn in Morgan and confess for a lesser charge."

"Sounds like a good deal to me," Nick said.

"It's a shit deal because he doesn't know where Morgan or the money is because he didn't steal anything."

"And why would I believe that?" Nick continued. "Maybe you want me to find him so you can shut him up before he can turn on your husband. If the police find him first, they'll offer him the same deal: turn on Stephen and get a lesser charge." Nick's face, weathered and serious, looked up into Holly's. His piercing blue eyes, youthful in comparison to the rest of his face, looked deep into Holly's. "Tell me how I know I'm not going to be an accessory to murder. Assure me that finding this Wood character is not a bad idea."

Holly held his gaze. She started to protest, to call him an asshole, to tell him this was a mistake. Then she broke down. Tears ran from her eyes, her face reddening. She cried hard and sobbed. "You know he's innocent. Don't you? Can't you tell? Isn't he on your list? I came here hoping—"

"Hoping what?" Nick asked, his scowl softening as he slid a box of tissues to Holly.

She took a tissue and dried her eyes. Her sobbing slowed. She took several deep breaths and looked up. "Hoping that you are who people say you are. That you're really him."

A slight smile came across Nick's face. "And who do people say I am?"

"That you're Santa Claus," Holly said.

Nick laughed. "Oh, ho, ho...you really are desperate."

Holly realized a drink was sitting next to her. *Jesus*, she thought, *how long was I crying?*

Nick lifted a glass to his lips and took a drink of rye whiskey. "Even if I was, did you think I could just pull Wood out of my bag, wrapped with a bow, and put him under the Christmas tree outside city hall? That I could pull some magical list out of my pocket and say, 'See here, Officer? Dash is innocent! He's on the nice list!' And that they'd just let him go?"

"I don't know. Maybe? I'm desperate, Nick. I don't care who you really are, if you can find Morgan...if you can believe Stephen is innocent. I feel so alone. So helpless. I guess I was hoping for a miracle, but I'd just be happy if you'd believe me and take the case just so I won't feel so alone."

Holly looked down. She picked up her drink. The glass felt heavy in her hand—and warm. *There's no way he had time to make a warm drink*, she thought. She smelled the drink, and her eyes closed. She suddenly remembered being eight years old. The family gathered at her grandmother's house every Christmas until she died. In fact, her eighth was the last Christmas with her grandma. She took a sip and knew immediately why she thought of Christmas with her grandma. "My grandmother always made mulled cider at Christmas..." Holly's voice trailed off as she opened her eyes. Her coat was laid neatly on the desk. On top was a rolled piece of paper tied with a red ribbon.

She unrolled the paper. Written with perfect penmanship and what appeared to be a quill pen was the following:

> To: Holly Dash
> From: Nick Saint
>
> Per our discussion, I will find Morgan Wood, CPA, and deliver him to the police. Whether or not he proves your husband's innocence is out of my control. My fees are $250 per day, plus incidental expenses with a minimum of five days' work. An additional $1,000 to be paid upon successfully delivering Morgan Wood to the police.

Miracles not included.

Sincerely,
Nick Saint

PS. Enjoy the cider. Please lock the door on your way out.

Holly looked up again. "Nick?" she called, but Nick was gone.

Chapter 2

By the time Holly realized Nick was gone, he was already in his car. He moved quickly toward the local gazette offices to meet up with a reporter who had been covering the Dasher of Dreams story. Rudy was a seasoned reporter with a knack for getting the story no one else could. On more than one occasion, this was with Nick's help. A number of years ago, Rudy was a young research assistant struggling to keep up with the often frenetic pace of journalism. He happened to cross paths with a private investigator who happened to be investigating the same case that Rudy was. They had a few drinks and exchanged notes. Nick provided valuable information, and Rudy became the star of the office. Rudy provided a key piece of information that helped Nick solve the case. From that time on, they saw fit to collaborate any time their professional paths happened to cross.

Rudy was waiting at the bar across the street from the paper when Nick arrived. Nick sat across from Rudy in a corner booth facing the door. Rudy pushed a White Russian across the table.

"It's no cookies and milk, I know." Rudy smiled.

Nick scowled. He hated Santa-related humor, especially when leveled at him.

"So what case brings Saint Nick to me today?" Rudy asked, though he could probably guess. Stephen Dash and the missing accountant were taking up most of his time and would be the only thing high profile enough for Nick to come to him first.

"I'm looking for the accountant, Wood," Nick began. "The papers only really say he's at large and the cops are looking for him.

I've got the impression that the second part may not be entirely true." Nick took a sip of his drink. "I'm guessing you know a lot more about it than made it to print."

Rudy took a big drag of beer. "Astute as always, Nick. And you don't know how much we left out. We kept it buttoned up at the request of the police, but there's tons of information about this guy." Rudy paused to take another drink.

"Any of it useful?" Nick asked.

"I don't know if it's useful, but it's unusual. And that, may in itself, be useful."

Nick's brow furrowed. He thought for a minute before relaxing his countenance. "So you don't think he's run off with the money then?"

"No, I think he's just running."

Chapter 3

Rudy had left a few hours ago, having handed Nick a large envelope containing all the information he had on the missing Morgan Wood. Nick sat in the bar, carefully studying everything Rudy had given him.

Morgan Wood was born on September 1, 1970, to parents Marvin and Linda, who both died on January 4, 1971. Morgan was placed into foster care until 1977 when his foster parents were arrested for child abuse. Morgan was sent to the St. Margaret of Cortana Orphanage. He resided there until his eighteenth birthday. He graduated with a decent GPA from high school and enrolled at the community college. After completing an associate degree in business, he worked as a clerk in an accounting firm. After a few years, he was admitted to the University of Michigan, where he completed his bachelor's and master's degree in accounting.

After sitting for his accounting license, Wood was recruited by Steale and Hyde, a large accounting firm with clients around the globe. Wood started with small local clients but quickly proved he had a talent for shoring up accounts, finding money through saving tax loopholes, and most importantly, building good relationships with clients. He quickly advanced to larger accounts, where his skills grew, as did his prestige within the company. Shortly after his thirty-sixth birthday, on September 21, 2006, he was offered a junior partnership, the youngest person to gain the title in company history.

Wood resided in a small apartment on the south side of town. Despite impressive earnings, he remained in his two-bedroom apartment that he'd lived in since first being hired by Steale and Hyde. He never married and, as far as anyone could tell, never dated anyone seriously. His proficiency at work may have come from the single-minded drive of a man without any distractions in his personal life. He had few hobbies anyone knew of aside from running. He was an avid runner and completed several marathons every year.

Sometime in 2010, Wood came into contact with Stephen Dash. Dash, a young and successful tax attorney, was looking for an accountant to help with a new charity that he was involved in. Steale and Hyde volunteered to provide the work free of charge and had asked Wood to get someone on it and to personally look after the account.

Wood took an interest in the cause and took on the account personally. He also began to volunteer with the charity outside work. Growing up as an orphan, Wood had very few happy Christmases. The Little Drummer Boy Charities collected money to provide holiday cheer to those that most need it, at-risk and orphaned children. In volunteering for the charity, Wood found something he never had before—family. He quickly fell in love with the work, the people, and the children. He began to use vacation time, all around Christmas, to see to it that the charity worked. Three years later, with Wood's help, Little Drummer Boy was a major charity. Wood left his six-figure salary and took a full-time job as the accountant for Little Drummer Boy.

Then Wood disappeared. On September 29, 2018, an audit was completed showing Wood and Dash had been diverting millions offshore over the course of several years. The day before the audit started, July 17, 2018, Wood placed a call to Stephen Dash. Dash did not answer, and Wood left a voicemail that, according to sources within the police department, simply said, "We're in trouble. We need to talk about this audit. Call me ASAP." The GPS device in Wood's phone showed he went to the parking garage, then left on foot. About three blocks later, his signal was lost. It never picked up again.

Nick ordered another drink. "Why would a successful man who had legally obtained wealth and prestige give it all up for something he was passionate about, then steal money, and run off?"

Nick was starting to see Rudy's point and began to see the same hole in Dash's case. Why should he give up a good job and a loving wife to rob some children and run off? *I suppose people do dumb stuff for money*, he thought, but still couldn't make sense of it.

Nick looked through the police reports Rudy had provided. "I'll never know how he gets these things."

Morgan Wood, forty-eight, male, Caucasian, 5'11" and 170 pounds, brown hair, brown eyes, scar on left cheek. No corrective lenses. No known tattoos. No previous criminal record. Person of interest in embezzlement of funds exceeding three million dollars from Little Drummer Boy Charities. Last known address: 1173 Carey Road, Apartment D. Drives a beige Honda Accord, 2003. Last seen parked at 12 Tower Way. Search of premises showed no matching vehicle. Security footage showed the car leaving at 1635 hours, heading south on Tower. No spouse or known significant other. No next of kin identified. Warrant for home still pending judicial authorization. Landlord had not seen or heard from the person of interest since July 1 when rent was paid by check in person, as was his usual habit. Bank records had been requested, awaiting judicial authorization. Potential coconspirator, Stephen Dash.

Nick finished his drink and paid his tab. He left the pub, stepping into a chill autumn wind. Nick took a deep breath and felt the cold air wash over his body. He punched 1173 Carey Road into the maps app on his phone and started toward his car.

Chapter 4

Nick arrived at Wood's apartment at five in the afternoon. He sat outside, observing the building, trying to figure out which apartment belonged to Wood. There was a single security entry point into the lobby. There were five floors with two apartments per floor. Apartment D would be on the third floor as there didn't appear to be any apartment's ground level. There was a balcony on each of the floors with access to a fire escape and sliding glass doors on each balcony to access the apartments. He noticed the apartment on the east side of the building had fresh flowers, a cold, hardy variety, maybe mums, that were well tended and thriving. There was a small table and two chairs. The west side was devoid of decoration, plant or otherwise. It also appeared unused in that there were no chairs, boxes, crates, cans, trash, or bicycles. None of the things he expected on a balcony were present. Knowing Wood was married to his work, it would not be surprising if he didn't use his balcony, but he had also been alone in the same apartment for years, and it seemed unlikely that he was not using his space fully. However, Wood had been gone for a few months, and Nick wasn't sure plants would thrive without help. As he was trying to decide which apartment may be Wood's, there was a knock on the passenger window.

Five kids, aged between six and ten, were standing outside, their mouths slightly open and wide eyes staring at Nick. He rolled down his window.

"What?" Nick asked, slightly annoyed by the interruption.

There was a long pause before the youngest asked, "Santa? Can I have a new football for Christmas?"

Nick laughed. "Do I look like Santa to you, Billy?"

The kids gasped. "It is you! You know my name!"

Shit, Nick thought, but he couldn't help it, not with kids anyway. It was hard not to be himself with them. "Look, kids, I'm not in the toy business anymore. Sorry."

It was like he'd let the air out of five child-shaped balloons. The kids slunk away. The youngest, Billy, put his key into the door at 1173 Carey Road. Nick honked the horn and yelled, "Billy! Wait up!"

Billy wasn't supposed to hold the door for anyone, not even a neighbor. It was a safety thing, or so his mom said. He was not sure about Santa though. Couldn't he get in anyway? Billy pulled the door shut and waited while Nick bounded to the door.

"Billy, can you let me in? I'm looking for a friend."

"Can't you just, you know…" Billy tried to make a gesture of a man sliding down a chimney, sliding a finger in and out of his closed hand in a very un-Santa-down-the-chimney gesture.

"Whoa, stop, stop," Nick said. "That's…no. Look, I can only do that on Christmas Eve. And let's not do that gesture again."

"Why?" Billy asked.

Nick wasn't sure if he meant the hand gesture or the chimney thing. "It's complicated. Christmas magic and all. Can you open up, please?"

Billy started for the door but stopped.

"What's wrong now?" Nick was getting impatient.

"I guess, I'm, just, well, not sure. I'm not supposed to open the door for strangers. And you're Santa Claus, but you said you don't do toys, so maybe you're not him?"

Nick sighed and closed his eyes. He took a deep breath. The wind picked up, carrying a scent of pine that filled the lobby of 1173 Carey Road. Frost edged across the glass doors. Nick opened his eyes and looked at Billy for a long minute.

"Stop shooting spitballs at Suzy and feed your goldfish. Listen to your mother. She works hard for you, and it's not easy on her own. Can you do that?"

Billy's wide eyes stared unblinkingly at Nick. He nodded.

"Good, now open the door and tell me what kind of ball you want."

Nick was outside Apartment D a few minutes later. "Damn kid, shaking me down for a ball." Interestingly, the apartment with the flowers was Apartment D. Nick thought about who was taking care of the plants. He looked at the door, a remnant of police tape still hanging to the frame. A red tamper seal on the door, still intact, marked the room as evidence.

"Who are you?" A woman's voice interrupted Nick's thoughts.

"Nick Saint. And you are?" Nick turned to see a woman, about forty years old, carrying four grocery bags.

"I'm Lucy. If you're looking for Morgan, he's clearly not there."

"Someone is taking care of his flowers," Nick replied.

"I know. It's me," Lucy replied.

"How?" Nick asked.

"I live upstairs. I take the fire escape." Lucy paused. "Who are you again?"

"Nick Saint. I'm a private investigator. I'm looking for Morgan."

"Why? Is there reward money or something?" Lucy asked.

"No, just another interested party hired me. Can I help you with your bags?"

Lucy looked at him for a minute. "Morgan didn't take any money. He loved that charity. Those kids were his purpose in life."

"I know. I want to help him prove it."

Lucy handed Nick two bags. "The cops locked the front door but didn't seal his balcony door. It's unlocked. You're welcome to come through my apartment and check it out."

Inside Lucy's apartment, Nick saw a photo of Morgan and Lucy. "Were you two, uh, close?" Nick pointed to the photo.

"Somewhat. We went on a few dates. Nothing came of it. There's something about him. He's pleasant and kind, but, I dunno, he's just not always there. You know?"

Nick nodded. "Did he tell you about his childhood?"

"No, not really. I know he lost his parents young. It's why he did the work at the charity. It's why he loved those kids."

"He suffered a lot. If he wasn't present, not always there with you, he had a good reason."

Lucy looked at Nick. "I know. I mean, I suspected something. Anyway, it doesn't matter now. I water all his plants because I bought most of them. Thought he'd like to make his home a little cheerier. That's how I knew the glass is open."

Nick thanked Lucy as he headed down the fire escape and into Morgan's apartment. Three things stood out as odd when Nick entered the apartment. First, it didn't smell unused. Unused spaces would begin to acquire smells. The accumulation of dust, the lack of air exchange, the lack of cooked foods with their oily aromatics no longer suffusing the space, the lack of sweat, the lack of cleaners, all add or subtract from a home's usual aroma. An unlived space would smell dead, not like death as was the case when the occupant died and the smell of their putrefying body filled the space, saturating every piece of furniture and carpet before leaking out into the greater world to announce the passing of a neighbor. No, not that kind of dead. The space smelled dead in that it was devoid of life. Even the smell of decomposing flesh at least carried the reminder that something was living there recently. A dead room smelled like nothing of a great and uneasy absence, which, Nick thought, was the reason people were so ill at ease in such a place. Somewhere deep down in their genes was a recognition that no life was to be found, that this was a place to be avoided if you want to live, and Morgan Wood's apartment did not smell dead.

Second, his power and utilities were all still on. The room, though not hot, was warm enough. He tested the tap and lights—all working—which was odd considering Morgan was not around to pay the bills.

Third, the place was in shambles. Every drawer opened and empty. Clothes, photo albums, files, furniture were all out of place. In any good police investigation such as this, everything would be searched. Evidence would be collected and carefully documented.

Sure, things might get messy, but the police were usually methodical. They stacked and organized to ensure no stone was left unturned. Yes, there was evidence of a methodical search, but there was also evidence of a more haphazard search on the home of Morgan Wood. Even stranger, the haphazard search appeared to have come after the first methodical search. Nick could see where the apartment had been turned out and sorted into piles of like items. Then some of those piles had been tossed around, as if someone was going through everything again and in a hurry.

Without access to the police reports and crime scene photos, Nick was going to have to try and piece together how the apartment looked before the police arrived. He walked through the living room which doubled as a dining room. The living room opened into a small but well-stocked kitchen. There was a half wall with a countertop separating the living and dining area from the kitchen. Nick turned right down a long, narrow hallway. A bicycle mount was on the wall but no bicycle. A key rack, repurposed to hold marathon finisher's medals, was next to the bike mount. Nick looked at the twenty-odd medals, primarily from the local marathon with a handful from nearby cities. A shoe rack underneath held several different types of athletic shoes—runners, cross-trainers, cycling. There were conspicuously open areas that likely once held additional shoes.

Turning around, Nick opened the door to the guest bedroom, which served as Morgan's study. A glass top desk with an expensive well-worn chair in the back corner, the only window just to the side, overlooked the alley below. His degrees were on the wall above the desk along with his accounting license. He had two computer monitors, a wireless keyboard, and a wireless mouse. There was a port where he could dock his laptop. A tall five-drawer filing cabinet stood just to the left of the desk. All the files were missing, no doubt taken wholesale by the forensics team to comb through. The closet in the room was small and along the wall opposite the desk. It was open and largely untouched. Summer weight jackets, shirts, shorts, cleaning supplies, and a vacuum cleaner took up the front of the closet.

Hung on the wall adjacent to the door were several framed pictures: a graduation photo from college and one from his first day at

Little Drummer Boy. Two empty picture hooks marked the location of missing pictures. Nick held his hand up to the wall, taking a rough measurement of the missing pictures based on a slight discoloration of the paint where the frame had hung.

Nick walked into the attached bathroom which was shared with the main suite. The bathroom, like the apartment, was small and quite disorderly, the contents of every drawer and cabinet having been disgorged and examined by the police. Looking around, Nick could tell that this mess was not made entirely by the police looking though Morgan's belongings.

Q-tips, floss sticks, and cold medicine were scattered on the floor and under the medicine cabinet. Nick opened the medicine cabinet. It was mostly empty. A few bottles remained on the shelf: hair gel, cologne, and seasonal allergy medicine. The toothbrush holder was empty, and his toothpaste was missing. Nick ran his finger along the top of the toothbrush holder. He could feel dried toothpaste around two of the openings.

"Either he uses two different spots for his brush or someone else was keeping their brush here." A small ring on the shelf marked where a bottle had been, possibly a prescription medication.

He passed into the main suite. The closet was open. Several nice suits were on hangers as well as his sweaters. There were a half dozen empty hangers between the suits and sweaters. Remembering the closet in the other room, Nick thought, *He rotates his clothes by season*, and noted there were no winter coats, sweatshirts, sweatpants, or jeans in the closet. All his shoes were in a pile, each apparently checked for hidden items. Several shoeboxes were upended on the floor, and their contents, stacks of pictures, were next to them.

Nick sifted through the stacks of photos. Most of these were from Wood's childhood or young adulthood, before every picture was digital and stored on the Cloud. He could find nothing recent among them. Nick stopped when he got to the fourth photo of Morgan taken from the same spot. In the photos, Morgan and a group of other children were seated outside a cabin near a lake.

"Whispering Pines Summer Camp," Nick read off the sign behind the group. The year was marked below along with a cabin number. Nick slipped the summer camp photos into his pocket. He moved on to the dresser drawers. Several had been emptied completely, likely socks, underwear, and warm clothes, if Nick were to guess.

Lucy heard a tap on her glass door, and she let Nick in. "Find anything?" she asked.

"Maybe," Nick said, walking to the picture of her and Morgan. He held his hand up to the frame, too big to be the missing photos.

"Were you ever in Morgan's office in his apartment?" Nick asked.

"Of course, it was the quickest way to the bathroom."

"Did you see any pictures on the wall that looked like this?" Nick pulled one of the summer camp photos from his pocket.

Lucy looked and thought for a minute. "Yeah, I did, but it was more recent. He was an adult."

"Who was he with?" Nick asked.

"No one. He was by himself, next to the cabin. It was more run-down though, like it hadn't been used for a while."

Nick thanked Lucy on the way to the door. As he was closing it, he stopped and turned, asking, "How much time are you spending down in Morgan's apartment?"

Lucy laughed. "His bills must be on autopay, which is why everything still works, including his Netflix account. I go down to watch TV."

Now it was Nick's turn to laugh. "Can't you change his log-in and then use his account from your apartment?"

Lucy looked down, embarrassed. "I'm saving money by using his Internet too."

"Oh, ho, ho." Nick laughed and headed off down the hall.

Chapter 5

Something awoke in the ancient forest. As the snow fell thick and fast, it shivered in its bed among the fir trees. It opened its eyes and looked around, waking as the twilight gave way to night. Its warm breath was condensing in the cold air. It shivered and stretched, yawning. The quiet of the long night was broken by a loud, piercing noise.

The sound of a ringing electronic alarm woke Nick from his dream. Nick rolled over in his bed and checked his phone. It was quarter after five. He rubbed his eyes. Stretching his back, there was a cacophony of cracks and pops as his spine rights itself. Fumbling in the dark, he found his lamp and turned it on. The sudden brightness caused him to shut his eyes, the white light of modern LED bulbs too much for his still-dark dilated pupils. "I always liked oil lamps better," Nick mumbled as he swung his legs out of bed.

After a quick shower, Nick slipped into his suit. It was one of a dozen in his closet, all the same: dark forest green with maroon pinstriping. A matching maroon necktie with full Windsor knot lay atop a crisp white shirt. A holly sprig cast in gold served as his tiepin. A silver reindeer rampant was pinned to his lapel. He wore boots, old and black, the leather polished but showed definite signs of being well-worn. The leather was scuffed, and the soles were thinning in spots. Nick thought of resoling them as he pulled the laces tight.

By 6:00 a.m., he was headed out into the still dark morning, his maroon trench coat and hat on the passenger seat. The GPS on his phone told him to turn right and head for the highway. He had a five-hour drive ahead of him.

After he got home the night before, Nick searched the Internet for the Whispering Pines Summer Camp. No website, no phone number. He did find several social media posts with old pictures, similar to the photo of Morgan he pocketed, with kids lined up outside cabins, smiling and enjoying being kids. Following a link tagged to one of these photos, he found that the owner, Gus Anderson, died at the age of eighty-six in late June. The funeral was held just after the Fourth of July holiday. The memorial page had hundreds of comments from previous campers, all well-wishing the family, all celebrating how Gus and his camp were the high points of their summers and young adult lives.

Whispering Pines was a summer camp for orphaned and at-risk youth. They came from all over to spend a few weeks doing normal things like singing, swimming, canoeing, hiking, roasting marshmallows, playing pranks, and having summer romances. Most importantly, Nick learned from the posts that they spent their summers in the company of other kids who were like them. At home, they may be outcasts or feel very alone. No one understood what it was like to not have a mom and a dad, but at Whispering Pines, everyone understood. No one laughed at the kid without parents. No one felt sorry for the kid from the foster home. At Whispering Pines, everyone had an equally tragic life, and no one cared. There, a kid could look past that sadness and be their true genuine self.

Nick spent a few hours combing through the comments, looking for any information that might be useful. Around midnight, he found a thread discussing the rumor of someone interested in buying Whispering Pines from Gus with the intention of reopening the camp.

There was no address or even city listed for Whispering Pines, but Gus's obituary said he died peacefully at home, never far from his beloved camp. Also from the obituary, Nick found that Gus was born and raised in the same town in which he died. The funeral home was there too. Nick had a hunch that Morgan was either the possible buyer of the camp or involved in the sale. And so Nick knew where he had to go.

Nick pulled into town around 11:45 a.m. He had topped off his tank about an hour outside town. He grabbed a few bags of chips, some water, and a cup of coffee. He was prepared to stake out the town, at least for a few hours.

The sleepy town of Trails End looked like something out of time. The closest big-box store was over an hour away. No major retailers, including chain grocers, had yet to come to town. Main Street was still lined with shops—a diner, a hardware store, a laundromat, and a green grocer. If it hadn't been for the cell phone store and check cashing establishment, Nick would've thought this place had kept itself out of the twenty-first century.

He turned off Main Street onto Elm and headed to the Martin Funeral Home. He pulled up outside. A funeral was underway.

Damn, that'll cost me some time, Nick thought as he pulled into a parking space in the funeral home lot. Nick had hoped to talk with the funeral director and get more information about Gus Anderson. He could go in under the guise of a bereaved friend to whoever was laid out for visitation and find the funeral director once inside, but Nick could not reconcile invading a funeral for personal gain. He could wait out the funeral and check in afterward, but there was no guarantee that anyone from the funeral staff would be available afterward to speak. Remembering the diner he saw on the way in, he decided the best move was to get some pie and, with any luck, chat up a local who might have information about Gus Anderson and Whispering Pines. Nick pulled out of the lot and turned back toward Main Street and the diner, Sandy's—home of the best pie this side of the Mississippi.

Nick parked across the street and dropped a quarter into the parking meter. He heard the click and buzz of the mechanical timer as it counted down his time. *Don't see these anymore*, Nick mused, smiling from the nostalgia.

Sandy's occupied the bottom floor of an apartment building. Inside, Nick counted thirty total tabletops, twenty of which were booths and ten freestanding tables. There was seating for six at the bar. A letter board menu hung above the counter, announcing the special of the day—open-faced turkey sandwich with cranberry sauce and mashed potatoes. Add pumpkin pie for one dollar. Next to the daily special was the pie list—pumpkin, cherry, blueberry, sweet potato, banana cream, key lime coconut cream, pecan, fudge, mixed berry, gooseberry, blackberry, raspberry, mint cream, peach ginger, peach, strawberry, and apple. A display case with slowly rotating shelves showed off the pies, already divided into slices and individually wrapped.

Nick sat at the counter next to a man of about sixty. He had dark tan and leathery skin. He wore a flannel shirt, well-worn jeans, and dirty boots. He was reading the local paper.

"Are you here for the funeral?" the man asked, not taking his eyes off the paper.

"No, sir, I'm not," Nick replied.

"What brings you to town then?"

"Business," Nick said as he ordered a coffee and picked up the menu.

"Not much business around here anymore," the man said as he closed his paper and took a hard look at Nick. "So what is it you are doing here?"

The bluntness could've been interpreted as rude by some, but Nick was familiar with this type of man. He had little time for small talk and saw no point in dancing around what you really wanted. If you want to know what business a stranger has in town, ask.

"I'm looking for the old Whispering Pines Summer Camp. Gus Anderson's place? I represent an interested buyer. Do you know it?" Nick looked the man in the eyes and held his gaze.

"I know it. I worked there a few summers as the groundskeeper. That was, oh, almost forty years ago. That got me started with my love of landscaping though. Now I run a landscaping company." He stopped to regard Nick before continuing, "What kind of buyer are you representing?"

Nick took a chance when he answered, "A property developer. We heard there are possible mine subsidence issues. We can't build if the lots aren't stable. Electronic records don't show any undermining, but we're worried about old or undocumented mines in the area. I'm meeting with someone from the historical society to go over old records. Cheaper to send me here to do a little digging than to drill core samples looking for abnormalities down below."

The man's eyes opened wide, but he didn't show any other emotion. "Property developer? What are you developing?"

"Well, I can't say exactly, but it would mean a lot of new landscaping opportunities." Nick could see he had the man's interest.

"Aw, hell, I can save you the trip. My family has been here for 150 years. There's never been any mining here. There's nothing but solid earth beneath your feet, especially over old Gus's place. Check the records if you like, but trust me, it's solid. And between you and me, I'm glad to be rid of that fella who wanted to reopen the camp. I heard he was wanted for some crime and disappeared. I heard the bank backed out of the deal."

Nick raised an eyebrow. "You don't say? A criminal wanted to open a summer camp? Was he from around here?"

"No, sir. We are an honest lot here. He was some big-city guy," the man said, drawing out the words *big* and *city*.

"And how did you hear about this?" Nick asked, taking a drink of his coffee.

"Well, it was in the news, but I first heard it from the detective who came here looking for him. Small town, you know. Word gets around." So he was not the only one thinking Morgan may have come here.

"Well, thank you for the information. I'll probably still check the records though since I'm getting paid to do it and all," Nick said as he tried to get the attention of the waitress to order.

"Good luck to you, Mr.?"

"Nick, Nick Saint."

"Nice to meet you, Mr. Saint. I'm Buck. If you need anything, give me a call." Buck handed Nick his business card, shook his hand, dropped a ten-dollar bill on the counter, and left.

Nick got the attention of Delores, the waitress serving the counter, and she took Nick's order for pecan pie. As he ate what was a truly exceptional piece of pie, Nick could feel eyes on him. He looked up to see an older woman, about seventy, if Nick had to guess, staring at him with daggers in her eyes.

"So you're the one looking to destroy our town?"

"I don't think so," Nick said, swallowing his bite of pie.

"You're either looking to build homes or big-box stores. Maybe both? Either way, that will be the end of our town and people like me. We're out of business. So I'll kindly ask you to leave now."

"I'm going to take a wild guess that you're Sandy," Nick said. He dropped a twenty on the counter.

"Damn right, I am," she said, hands on her hips.

"Excellent pie, by the way. I really enjoyed the bit I had."

"Great. Now get out."

Nick wandered down the street. He stepped into the hardware store. Inside, there was an old photo of Whispering Pines while the cabins were still being built.

"That's my grandfather," a man said, pointing a finger to the photo. "He and Gus built that place in 1958. Gus had a vision for the camp. He'd seen plenty of orphans and displaced children during the war. Knowing there were so many here in the states... Well, he had to do something. My grandfather was a jack-of-all-trades. He could do just about anything, and he did just about everything. His grandfather started this store in 1908. Grandpa was working the store by 1958, but he had a son on the way, my father, and he needed the extra cash. So he spent his weekends building the cabins and outbuildings for Gus."

Nick turned to the man. "I'm just passing through town. I thought I might stretch my legs a little. Thanks for the history lesson though. Is the camp still around?"

"Unfortunately, no. Gus passed not long ago, but he had retired and shut the camp down years ago. Someone wanted to buy it but...," he trailed off.

"But what?" Nick asked.

"Well, something came up, I guess. It doesn't matter. But the rumor is some property developer is nosing around now. My little shop's days may be numbered."

Nick shook his head and thought, *News really does travel fast around here.* "That's too bad," Nick said. "Was it close by? Maybe on my way out of town, I could drive past. Give me something to look for besides cattle and trees?"

"Sure, it's only a few miles away. I can give you directions." The shopkeeper took out a pen and the back of a discarded receipt and drew a map. Nick thanked him and headed back to his car.

*****

The small town quickly receded into farmland. Cows in pasture and fields plowed under alternating with winter wheat. Occasional houses and barns drifted past. Twenty minutes out of town, Nick spotted the turn onto a gravel road. Whispering Pines Lane wound down a small valley. The tree-lined lane spilled into a large parking lot, no doubt intended to handle busloads of children.

The main building looked worse for the wear with sections of the roof sagging and shingles missing. The windows were boarded up, and the door was padlocked shut. There was some graffiti on the walls, mostly the initials of local teenage lovers professing their devotion to one another. Empty cans of cheap beer were scattered about. The medical and administrative offices were close by and seemed to have fared better. Their roofs were intact with fewer beer cans on the ground. Through the nearly leafless trees, Nick could see the lake and boathouse. He took a walk down an overgrown but still clearly visible trail.

A few hundred yards away, just out of sight of the road and main camp area, were twelve cabins in two rows of six. Unlike the building out front, these buildings were still in pristine condition, as were the surrounding grounds. Apparently, teenage love and bravery stopped where the dark walk through the woods to the cabins began. Each cabin had a name that corresponded with a local native tribe: Iroquois, Seneca, Algonquin, and so on. *Probably his ancestors took this land from one of these people*, Nick sighed as he thought of the irony. The last cabin on the left bearing the name "Wyandot" looked familiar. Nick pulled one of the pictures out of his pocket and held it up. It was undoubtedly the same cabin from the photos.

Nick walked around the cabin, looking for signs of recent activity. He saw none. No disturbed dust. No pried open windows. No footprints other than a small rodent. No loose locks. Everything looked like it was shut years ago and never touched again. Nick checked the remaining cabins but found no trace of anyone else there. He wandered the grounds for an hour, checking for signs of human activity. The drained pool, the chapel, the barn, and the toolshed were all free of traces of recent human activity. At the lake, the boathouse was a crumbling mess. Moisture and termites got the best of a few support pillars, and the center of the roof had collapsed, breaking a window and knocking open the door. When the wind blows, it caused the door to open and shut. The slow, loud *clap, clap, clap* of the wooden door on its frame echoed into the silence of the lake.

Nick sat on a stump at the water's edge. He watched the water. The rippling surface showed the wind as it blew across the surface. The floating dock bobbed with the waves. He looked for jumping fish or frogs, but at this time of year, the lake felt dead. He picked up a stone and skipped it. He picked up another and then another. Bending down for a fourth stone, he saw it—a heel print. He looked around and found the partial imprint of a running shoe. Then another. And another. Then nothing. Nick followed the shore for some distance, picking up shoe prints here and there, going in both directions around the lake. Judging from the width of the stride and estimated size of the shoe, an average-height man was running when he made the prints, Nick thought.

Halfway around the lake, Nick stopped cold. The hair on his neck stood up. He turned only his head but saw nothing. Still, he felt unseen eyes upon him. He slowly turned around but couldn't see anyone or anything. Weighing his options, Nick headed back to the cabins, never feeling at ease during the walk. That primal instinct of being watched never disappeared. Passing the cabins, he stopped.

Pulling a pen from his coat, he wrote on the back of one of the photos he took from Morgan's apartment:

> Nick Saint, PI
> I don't think you stole anything. I want to help. Call me at 555-0101.

Nick tucked the photo into the door of the "Wyandot" cabin and walked back to his car. Driving away slowly, he swore he could see someone in the trees watching the cabins from the lake.

Chapter 6

On his way back to town, Nick decided to find Gus Anderson's house. It was not likely that a man on the run would squat in the home of a recently deceased acquaintance. The likelihood of a family member or an executor of the estate trying to clear the home and sell it would be quite high.

It was almost five when Nick got back into town. He parked on a side street just off Main Street. As he was getting out of his car, he heard a voice calling from across the street.

"Hey, stranger! I thought you were just passing through?" Nick recognized the hardware store owner's voice.

"I was, but I took a walk around the campground. Thanks, by the way, for the directions. Anyway, I lost track of time. The lake is beautiful this time of year. By the time I was ready to hit the road again, it was already starting to get dark. It'll be a really late night if I try to push on to my next destination, and I'm just not as good at driving at night as I used to be. So I thought I'd come back to town for dinner and hopefully find a place to stay. Got any suggestions?"

"If you like pie, you can't go wrong with Sandy's. Best pie around. The rest of her menu is okay too."

"I'm a diabetic," Nick lied as he crossed the street to continue the conversation.

"Okay, no pie. Well then, I'd suggest the Oakwood Inn. The food is good, and they have an excellent beer selection. I'm not sure if that's on the menu as a diabetic though. I'll be honest, I don't know much about that particular affliction."

"It's okay." Nick laughed. "Neither do I."

The man laughed and continued, "As far as lodging...well, the nearest decent hotel is just off the interstate, about thirty minutes from here."

"How about something less than decent here in town? Anything where I won't get Norman Bates'd or charged by the hour would do just fine."

"There's the Royal, about five minutes from here, on the other side of town where Main Street turns back into a four-lane highway. It's old. The tubs are stained from the hard water. The carpets are musty, and the rooms smell like old cigarettes. The beds are lumpy, and I wouldn't use the ice machines, but the sheets are clean. They've got hot water with good pressure in the shower, and there's always a few rooms available."

"Sounds like you've spent a night or two there," Nick said, raising an eyebrow. "Has your wife ever kicked you to the couch?"

"Sure, who hasn't been?" Nick smiled.

'Well, my wife won't allow feet or heads on our couch. She doesn't want to ruin the fabric."

"So she kicks you to a shitty motel?"

"It's either that or pitch a tent in the yard."

Nick thanked him for the advice, and they shook hands. Then Nick started walking toward the Oakwood Inn.

Nick thought he may be getting spoiled by city living. What passes for decent food in this town was disagreeable to his palate, and a good beer selection in this town meant they have the full range of Miller products. Still, he was glad for a hot meal and a cold beer.

As promised, the Royal had rooms available. They did smell of mildew and smoke. The bed was lumpy, and the stained tubs did have hot water. In its day, the Royal likely lived up to its name. Built in the late '40s, just after the Second World War, the Royal would have been a booming a business. The now-growing middle class, kids in tow, were hitting the open road in search of rest and relaxation. The family in a sedan or wagon, rumbling down the old highways, Ike's interstates not yet built, would find ample need of these roadside motels. After the interstate highways were completed, places like the Royal lost most of their business. It was a wonder that a town such as Trails End was able to provide enough business to keep the Royal open.

Nick pulled out his phone and connected to the Wi-Fi. He checked the local county assessor website, looking to find the name of the current owner of Whispering Pines. According to the site, the camp is situated on two hundred acres. Among the various buildings listed was a farmhouse. Looking at the survey maps, the house was on the opposite end of the property from the campground. The current owner was a Sandra Wescot, but there were liens on the property. Gus must have fallen behind or simply forgot to pay his property taxes for a number of years.

Nick opened the obituary for Gus. "Survived by Sandra Wescot, née Anderson, his niece." He did a quick search for Sandra Wescot and Sandra Anderson but came up empty. Whoever she was, she was not listed and didn't have a public social media presence.

On a hunch, Nick checked the nightstand. There, he found a phone book. *I didn't even know they made these anymore*, he thought. He opened to the *W*s: Walter, Waldo, Wescot, Sandra Wescot. He checked the time. It was after eleven. He keyed the number into his phone, saved the contact, and fell asleep.

It was early when Nick woke the next morning. He showered and dressed in a clean suit. He learned from experience that a case could take unexpected turns. Having twice been caught out of town with nothing clean to wear, once covered in cow manure and once forced to turn over the shirt on his back as evidence to the police, Nick now kept a travel bag packed and in his trunk at all times. "Say what you will about the Boy Scouts," Nick had said as he put the bag together, "but that 'be prepared' motto is good advice."

He half-heartedly looked for a room service menu but couldn't imagine one existing. He rang the front desk. After eight rings, he was about to hang up when a sleepy voice answered.

"Royal front desk." The desk clerk yawned. "How may I help you?"

"Ah, yes, this is Nick in room 8. I was wondering about breakfast at this hour. Anything open in town?"

There was another long yawn on the other end. "Sure, Nick. Sandy's opens at 6:00 a.m. Also, the Gas and Go is open twenty-four hours. They have a sandwich shop. The coffee is so-so, but the food is not too bad."

"Thanks. I think I'll try the Gas and Go. I need to top off my car anyway."

Nick hung up, and the phone rang again almost immediately. Nick answered.

The front desk clerk replied, "Mr. Saint? This is the front desk again. There seems to be a letter here for you."

Nick picked up the letter at the front desk and took it with him. He bought gas, a mediocre breakfast sandwich, and a cup of coffee that tasted like it has been on the warmer for a few hours. He pulled over in the parking lot of a not-yet-open dollar store. He took a pocketknife out and carefully sliced open the envelope. Neatly printed in big block letters on the outside of the envelope were the words, "Mr. Nick Saint." Inside was a single sheet of paper folded in thirds. Nick unfolded the paper and found a telephone number and a time. He checked his watch, a 1950's Smith's Deluxe wristwatch. The time was 7:30 a.m. He had forty-five minutes to kill before he was to call the number on the paper. He decided to key the number into his phone and then drive around town. When he was done entering the number, his jaw dropped. "I'll be damned." The number was that of an existing contact in his phone—Sandra Wescot.

The call was answered on the third ring, precisely at 8:15 a.m., but Nick heard no one on the other end. "Hello? Is anybody there?" Nick asked.

"First, you're a land developer, here snooping about my property. Then you're a detective leaving cryptic notes around my property. And if I were to believe the Internet, which I don't, you're Father Christmas himself! So which is it? Who are you, and what are you doing here?"

The voice sounded familiar. "Is this Sandy from the diner?" Nick asked.

"I asked you first," she replied. The annoyance in her voice was a definitive yes to Nick.

"I am not a property developer. I am a detective. I'm looking for the man in that picture I left at the cabin. I was hired to find him, and, truth be told, I think he's on your uncle's land."

At this last remark, Sandy snorted. "Hmph…first of all, that is my land. Uncle Gus died and left it to me. I am having some legal issues currently. The damned state feels that because Gus owed some back taxes that I can't pay, they can just take it from me. But it's mine! Mine to do with as I please."

"Fine, it's your land. I don't really care about that anyway. I'm looking for Morgan Wood. Do you know where he is?"

There was a long silence—long enough that Nick began to think she hung up.

"Morgan is a good man. He was friendly and kind to my uncle. He'd done well for himself despite his upbringing. He always told us Gus was part of the reason why. He'd call and write to Gus. When Gus died…" Sandy paused. She held back tears and continued, "When Gus died, I inherited his land and his debt. I don't know why he didn't pay his bills, but he didn't have much left in his bank when he died. I was devastated when I realized I'd lose the property. I planned to retire there."

She paused, and Nick asked, "What about your restaurant?"

"What about it? I do a fine business, but restaurants work on a narrow margin. And in this slowly dying town? It's razor thin."

"I heard Morgan was going to buy Gus's place. Is that true?"

"No, he wasn't. He wanted to reopen the camp. He wanted to propose to the Little Drummer Boy board that they purchase the camp. Let it do for at-risk kids what it did for him."

"How'd you feel about that?"

"Morgan was going to ask that the camp be purchased and reopened but a fifteen-acre plot and Gus's home be left to me. He wanted me to have the retirement I wanted. I loved the idea. And then this whole mess…"

This time she paused, Nick could tell she was crying. He let her go until she could start again, having gained her composure.

"It's all gone to hell now. And like I told the other guys, I don't know where Morgan is now."

That caught Nick by surprise. "Other guys?"

"Cops, I think," Sandy said. "They wore cheap suits. They drove a rental. I forgot their names. They came not long after Morgan disappeared. They spent a few days in town then left."

Nick thought long and hard about this—long enough that it was Sandy's turn to think Nick may have hung up. "Morgan's your friend. I get that. But I'm not trying to find him to lock him up. I think he's innocent. I want to clear this whole mess up for him. I can give you that retirement you want, if you trust me," he said.

"So you really think you're Saint Nick after all." Sandy laughed. "Will you leave the deed under the Christmas tree all wrapped up with a bow?"

Nick smiled. "I could, but I'm pretty sure you'll have to go to the tax collector to sign some papers first."

Sandy hung up without ever acknowledging she knew anything about Morgan Wood. She did invite Nick over for pie. The diner closed at 9:00 p.m. He was to arrive at 9:30 p.m. He went back to the Royal and took a nap. If all went well, he was hoping to have a plus one for an all-night drive back to the city.

The sound of a car crash startled Nick. He was walking down the nearly empty Main Street toward Sandy's when the sound of squealing tires followed by a hollow *thud* and crunch echoed from the alley that ran parallel to Main Street behind the buildings of the main thoroughfare. Three staccato bursts and a second squeal of tires sent him running. A dark blue or gray sedan erupted from the alley onto Main Street, its lights off and laying rubber well onto Main before disappearing into the night.

As Nick rounded the corner, he could hear the screams of a woman. Arriving a moment later, he could see Morgan Wood lying on the ground next to the open passenger door. Sandy Wescot, still behind the wheel, was screaming. Steam was rolling from under the collapsed hood. Nick reached through the open passenger door and put the car in park before he turned off the engine. Sandy looked at Nick, tears running down her face.

Nick could hear the sirens in the distance and the wail of a firehouse whistle alerting the local volunteers to an emergency. The

Chapter 7

After a long night of waiting at the local sheriff's office, Nick was finally interviewed and released by the state police detectives. Twice now, he had to leave his clothes for evidence. After he tested negative for gunshot residue—he did not and had never owned a weapon—the detectives chose to believe his version of events and let him go. Sandy was taken to the county trauma center. She was mostly bruised but had two fractured ribs. At her age, she was at high risk for pneumonia, so she was going to be observed closely for a few days. She later confirmed Nick's story for the detectives. She may be in some legal trouble for hiding Morgan as he was wanted by the police, but given the circumstances, she was likely to face no real consequences.

Nick showered at the Royal and then checked out. *If you are who I think you are*, Nick turned this phrase over and in his mind, *you'll know where to find it.* He really wished he had more to go on, but he couldn't sit in his car sipping bad gas station coffee all day. Sandy's was closed, of course, so the Gas and Go had to do for breakfast.

Nick pulled the map back up on his phone and plotted a route to Gus Anderson's house. Twenty minutes later, he was looking through the window of a locked garage. Morgan's car was parked under a coat of dust. He looked through the front window and could already tell he was not the first to visit. Going around back, the glass to the kitchen door was busted out, the door unlocked. Nick entered and tried the switch. The power was off. Either Morgan was off the grid completely or he was staying somewhere else.

The house was mostly empty. The furniture and appliances, gone and photos, gone. Judging by the dust patterns on the floor, a few stacks of boxes that had been in the corner of the living room were now open, their contents strewn about. Mostly, it was old documents, bank statements, personal correspondence, and the like. These boxes were likely slated for shredding or, given the rural setting, the burn pile.

At the top of the stairs, Nick checked the bedrooms. The guest room was empty. The master bedroom had a few more opened boxes, the contents similar and similarly scattered about. He went down in the basement, using the small flashlight he always carried, but it, too, was completely empty.

Outside the house, he sat on a bench next to a firepit. He looked out into the gray sky and to the forest in the distance, now almost completely barren, only a few leaves still holding on. A gentle breeze rustled the crisp leaves and branches of the oak in the yard. The smell of decaying leaves was strong, and there was a hint of woodsmoke in the air from a far-off chimney. Nick stood up and turned to head back into the house. In the living room, he headed straight for the fireplace. He got down on one knee and shone his light up into the chimney. The soot was thick but recently disturbed. "Oh, ho, ho, ho." Nick laughed.

Nick was speeding down the back roads, his eight-cylinder engine screaming as he tried to put some distance between him and Whispering Pines. It would add two hours to the trip, but he wasn't taking any interstates or main roads back to the city. He checked the time. He'd be back in town by 8:30 p.m. He called Rudy.

"Saint Nick! To what do I owe the pleasure of your call?"

"Do you know if the police recovered a computer from Morgan Wood?"

"As far as I know, they had his computer, and the police forensics unit was looking at copies of the server from Little Drummer Boy. Why?"

"What about a laptop? Or any drives?"

"Why?" Rudy asked. "Have you found one?"

Nick paused. "I haven't found a laptop, but I saw a docking port for one. He had a home office setup."

"You were in his apartment?" Rudy asked in mock astonishment. "No, no laptop I know of was recovered. Isn't his house still a crime scene?"

"Maybe. I wouldn't know. I didn't go through the front door. Have you heard the news?" Nick asked.

"I write the news." Rudy laughed then turned serious. "Wait… what news?"

"Morgan Wood is dead. Murdered last night."

Rudy couldn't ask questions fast enough. Nick answered just as quickly.

"A small town called Trails End. Nine thirty last night, he was shot in the chest. I was there. I saw the shooter's car take off. There was one witness, Sandra Wescot. She's in county general. Minor injuries from a car crash. Rudy, I need you to find out if the shooter took anything from the scene. I'm guessing they took his laptop."

"If they took his laptop, there must've been evidence on there. Something that someone didn't want seen," Rudy said as he furiously wrote down what Nick told him.

"Yeah, no shit, Rudy. But why kill him? Unless he knew the who and what that someone didn't want seen."

"So you do think he was set up? That he was a fall guy?" Rudy asked.

"I think whoever is behind this didn't count on the accountant to get away with his laptop. I'm guessing they covered their tracks electronically, but when the accountant and his laptop disappeared, there was no way to tell if his computer was connected to the system. He could have had an old untampered version of the data. If he analyzed it…maybe he could prove who did it."

"That's definitely worth killing for," Rudy said. "What's your next move, Nick?"

"The cops have one set of my clothes, and the ones I'm wearing are covered in soot. I'm going to get clean, and then I'm going to see my client."

"So you're off to see Holly Dash?"

"She and her husband have the most to gain from Wood's death. And she owes me my fee since I found Wood."

"Be careful, Nick. I'll find out about the laptop. And thanks for the tip about Wood."

Chapter 8

Nick pulled into town around eight. He'd driven hard and needed to rest. He pulled into the lot by his office. He headed for Paddy's to get a drink and something to eat.

"You look like hell, Nick," Paddy said.

"You're not looking so good yourself, Paddy." Nick laughed.

"Your usual?" Paddy asked.

Nick nodded and went to the restroom. He washed his face and hands, the soot staining the sink. Back at the bar, there was a cold beer, a double rye, and venison shepherd's pie waiting.

After filling his belly and getting another drink, he paid his tab and headed to the door. He turned off his phone and took the bus across town. He walked the final few blocks, making sure he wasn't being followed. Satisfied he was alone, Nick headed home. He collapsed into bed and slept late into the next morning.

Showered and in a fresh suit, Nick headed back across town to his car. Nick pulled into the long winding drive leading up to the home of Mr. and Mrs. Dash just after three in the afternoon. He parked outside the detached three-car garage. Inside the garage, there was just one car, a 2012 gray Mercedes. There was an empty spot where another car may have been parked at one time and a third bay half full of moving boxes.

Nick continued to the front door and rang the bell. While he waited, Nick looked over the recently renovated home. The original building was a mid-nineteenth-century farmhouse. Now fully renovated, the home had modern windows, a sizable addition, and a large wraparound porch that overlooked an impressive lawn that was hidden from the road by old growth pine. The home was situated on ten acres and included a barn and stable. There were several meadows and a few acres of forest. The fields were enclosed by new white-wood rail fencing. From the realty app on his phone, Nick knew this was a million-dollar investment even before the upgrades.

He rang a second time, and he heard footsteps echoing in a long empty hallway. Unlike the crisp click of heels that had preceded his client at the outset of the case, these footfalls were muted and shuffling. The Holly Dash who greeted Nick at the door was not the same woman he met in his office. Her hair was down in a loose ponytail. She was wearing sweatpants and a sweatshirt with a pair of well-worn running shoes on her feet. There were bags under her bloodshot eyes. She wasn't wearing makeup or jewelry, not even her wedding ring. Her hunched shoulders lifted when she saw Nick, and a smile creeped across her face.

"Have you found him?" she asked, the hope evident in her voice.

"I found him, but…can I come in?" Nick replied. Her shoulders slumped once again, and the smile faded.

"But what, Nick?" she asked.

"He's dead. Murdered on his way to meet me. We need to talk. May I come in?"

Tears streamed down her face as she moved to the side, inviting Nick in. He followed her through the empty foyer of fresh-laid marble that extended down the hallway. The bare white walls of the home echoed the sound of her shuffling steps and the heavy sound of his boots.

"I'd offer you a seat in the great room," she said, gesturing to a high-ceiling room with a large stone fireplace, flanked by floor-to-ceiling windows that looked across a meadow to the forest, "but as you can see…no furniture."

She turned and headed into the kitchen. There was a breakfast bar with a few tall stools. "May I?" Nick motioned to a stool, and she nodded.

Nick took a seat and said nothing. Holly put a kettle on the stove and excused herself. She returned as the kettle began to sing.

Her bloodshot eyes were now a solid red and swollen. She had been crying. However, she was now composed and poured two mugs of tea. She stood opposite Nick, cradling the hot mug in her hands.

"We sunk a lot into this place. It was our dream home." She paused and sipped her tea. "We bought mostly new furniture, but we put it on our credit card. Our accounts have all been frozen. All deliveries held. I'm all alone in this big empty house, and I have to sit on the floor. We kept our old mattress so at least I have somewhere to sleep. I guess I'm lucky for that. I'm not sure how long the bank will let me stay here. Maybe when the power goes out, I'll just fade away with it." She sipped her tea. "So what happened to Morgan?"

"I found him. I invited him to meet me. From the little I knew about him, I didn't think he was a thief. He just didn't seem the type."

Holly snorted.

"Am I wrong?" Nick asked. "What haven't you told me?"

"Nothing. It's just…Stephen, he didn't embezzle that money. I know it. The only other person who could've done it was Morgan. He's the only one."

Nick thought for a moment. "Say you're right. He did do it, and he was the only one who could have. Then who murdered him? And why?"

Holly said nothing, and Nick continued, "He was coming to meet me and was shot dead. I don't know who killed him, but I am willing to bet it was because he knew who stole the money or, at the very least, because he could prove who didn't."

They sat quietly for a few minutes while sipping their tea.

"This is a very nice house, Holly. Very expensive, I'd guess. I know your husband makes a decent living, but I didn't think it was decent enough to afford all of this." Nick stared at Holly.

Her sadness turned to anger. "I'm not sure I like what you're insinuating, Mr. Saint, but if I were you, I'd choose my next words carefully."

"What aren't you telling me, Holly? How can you afford all of this? You are, as far as I can tell, a socialite. You don't work, and your husband is not making the kind of money you need for a place like this. Morgan Wood died, I think, because he knew something about this missing money. Something someone wanted to be kept quiet. Your husband is in jail. Your accounts are frozen. With Wood dead, your husband is the only suspect that can be charged for the embezzlement. Without his accomplice, there might not be enough evidence to convict him. He might get away with it."

There was fire in Holly's eyes. She slammed her mug down on the countertop, breaking it. "Get out!" she roared, dragging Nick by his coat sleeve toward the door.

"Or...," Nick said, and Holly stopped.

"Or what?"

"Or Stephen and Morgan were both set up. They were to take the fall for someone else, and they didn't count on Morgan disappearing. They didn't know what he knew, but the fact that he wasn't arrested and disappeared after trying to warn your husband probably meant he knew something. With Morgan dead, your husband is the only one to take the fall. But who and why? Why set anyone up at all? If you're good enough to set this all up, to fake the data, why not just hide it better or just disappear with the money when the audit comes?"

Holly was still holding onto Nick's coat but had stopped short of the door. "So you don't think Stephen did it?"

Nick shook his head. "Your husband was already on the hook for the embezzlement. Even without Wood, there's a pretty strong case against him. If Wood could prove himself innocent, it would have just left your husband in the same position. He had nothing to gain except possibly a murder charge."

Holly let go of Nick's sleeve.

"So, Holly, I'll ask again. What aren't you telling me? Where did the money come from for the house? And who would benefit from your husband losing everything?"

Holly sighed. She rubbed her eyes. She was tired. "Stephen had some money in a trust. I've known about it since we were married. He never touched it, said it was for retirement. He wanted us to travel and enjoy our golden years."

"Then what happened?" Nick asked.

"Last year, Stephen said we should build our dream home, spend his trust. I asked him why. What about our retirement? He told me we were taken care of and to not worry about it. I know now how that sounds, but at the time…we had money, Nick. Plenty. Why steal more and risk everything? We had enough. Whatever his reason, it was legal. As for who could benefit? I have no idea."

Nick closed his eyes and breathed deeply. The wind outside suddenly picked up, whistling through the rails of the porch. The front door blew open, and then the wind calmed as the scent of pine filled the foyer. Nick put on his hat and adjusted it just how he liked it. He straightened his coat. He turned and walked out the front door.

Holly called after him, "That's it? Not even a goodbye?"

Nick called over his shoulder, "Goodbye, Mrs. Dash."

Holly could hear Nick's car come to life and pull down the long driveway. She headed back to the kitchen. There, on the counter, was a rolled piece of paper with a red ribbon next to her unbroken mug. With a trembling hand, she opened the roll. It read:

> To: Holly Dash
> From: Nick Saint
>
> Consider this an extension of our previous contract. All prior fees still apply. Payment upon completion of my investigation.
>
> Sincerely,
> Nick Saint
>
> PS. Consider the couch a gift.

Holly put down the note. "What couch?" She looked into the great room, not sure what to expect and felt disappointed to see the same empty room. She jumped at the sound of the doorbell. Outside, she could hear a delivery truck idling.

Chapter 9

"Children don't lie," Nick once told Rudy.

"Maybe you really are just Nick Saint, a crabby-assed old PI," Rudy said. "Because Santa Claus, the real Saint Nick, would certainly know that children lie. I submit my four-year-old as exhibit A."

"Rudy." Nick laughed. "I know kids tell lies. 'I didn't eat all those cookies. No, I didn't draw on the wall. I never touched my brother! I have no idea why he's crying.' I know all about that. I mean, they can't lie to me. I can read their hearts. It's a gift or maybe a curse. Jury is still out on that. My point is kids don't lie deep down. They can't hide their true nature from me."

"And why is that, Nick?"

"Because, unlike adults, children haven't learned to lie to themselves and believe those lies. Sadly, most adults lie, even to themselves. And that hides their true heart away, even from me."

Nick thought about this on the way home from the Dashes' house. Holly's heart wasn't completely hidden. She believed in her husband. She truly believed in his innocence. Still, she was hiding something, maybe even from herself.

It was late when Nick got home, but he decided to take a look at the data from the thumb drive. He found a jumble of files: copies of QuickBooks, spreadsheets, staff schedules, and bank transfers. After an hour, he closed down his computer.

Shit, he thought. *I was hoping he would have left me a letter explaining all of this.*

Nick realized two things as he was falling asleep. One, he was going to need time to sort through all of this material. Two, even if he did figure out what Morgan did, it was just copies of files. Maybe a good computer forensics team could figure out where it came from, but without the laptop it was copied from, it was circumstantial evidence at best. This would only guide his investigation. Whatever was on that drive would not exonerate Stephen Dash.

Monday came and went. Nick spent the day scanning the files he found and generally being bored to tears by the sheer volume of data.

God bless the bean counter, he thought as his eyes, strained from his day's labors, closed while he sipped a drink. *Chalk up another mundane Monday.*

The Tuesday newspapers were, by and large, as boring as Monday had been except for the announcement of Stephen Dash's upcoming arraignment hearing. Apparently, the death of Morgan Wood, the investigation of which was still ongoing, lit a fire to arraignment and moved toward a trial for Stephen Dash.

Aside from this piece of news, Tuesday played out much like Monday had with Nick collating and sorting reams of data. Nick slept that night with the satisfaction of having at least made sense of the mess of files and could now analyze the data in a methodical way. Wood, he theorized, hid the copy before he knew what was on it, before he could organize and analyze it.

Wednesday was the first real news of the week. Nick found out Stephen Dash was being charged with a felony in the first degree. If convicted, he could be facing serious jail time. He also learned all assets of the Dashes were to remain frozen. Stephen Dash's law firm let him go, and his law license was suspended. His firm, wanting to distance from the case, vowed to not provide any legal advice to Stephen.

In other words, Nick thought, *he's being hung out to dry.* Stephen Dash would be released to house arrest until the trial. *At least I can talk to him now*, Nick thought.

Nick moved to his office on Wednesday, partly for the change of scenery and primarily for the proximity to Paddy's. He needed a decent meal and a good drink. Nick had just finished the paper when his phone rang. It was Rudy.

"Nick," Rudy began, "care to take a walk?"

Nick had known Rudy for a while. He never called him Nick, and they never took walks.

"It's 11:30 a.m.," Nick said. "I was thinking about lunch. Care to join me?"

There was a long pause. Nick could tell something was up.

"I was hoping we could walk, Nick." Rudy sounded nervous.

"Okay. Let's walk. Anywhere in particular you'd like to go?"

"Meet me in thirty minutes, Riverfront Park, by the boathouse."

*****

Rudy and Nick walked in silence for ten minutes. Finally, away from anyone they could see and with the river to one side and train tracks to the other, Rudy started talking.

"First off, you were right about the laptop or I think you are. Sandy Wescot saw Wood with a computer when she brought him food. She had been hiding him. He had a briefcase with him when he was shot. The shooter took the bag. Sandy was dazed and didn't get a good look at the shooter. She hasn't been back to where Wood was hiding. She was still in the hospital, but he probably brought the laptop."

"Okay. I'll assume the shooter has it. You couldn't tell me this on the phone?"

"Nick, my contact at the police department said they have a ballistics report already on the bullets that hit Wood. The bullets were from a gun connected to two other murders."

"So the shooter is a pro?"

"No, Nick, he's a cop. Maybe."

"What? How do they know that?"

"The gun was in an evidence locker up until, well, until it killed Wood. The gun was evidence in a case that was closed when the suspect died. It was to be destroyed later this year with a bunch of other weapons."

"That's not good."

"No, Nick, it's not."

Nick and Rudy walked in silence back to their cars. Rudy headed back to his office, and Nick headed to Paddy's for a stiff drink.

Chapter 10

Nick woke on Thursday morning with his head a little clearer than the night before. He had sat quietly, contemplating late into the night, trying to make sense of the case, but could come up with no plausible explanations. After coffee and toast, he showered, dressed, and headed back to his office. He picked up his papers from the newsstand on the corner and went inside. He started in on his papers hoping to clear his mind by thinking of something else, but he couldn't concentrate. The case was looming in his mind, crowding out all other thoughts.

He pulled out a notepad and wrote out what he knew. One, Wood ran the day before the audit and disappeared. Two, Wood found something but never turned himself in to prove his innocence. Why? Three, a gun stolen from a police evidence locker killed him. Four, Stephen Dash had money and a good job but started spending big recently. His wife claimed he said they were taken care of but by who and how? Five, any proof or clues was likely in that thumb drive Wood left for Nick.

Nick rubbed the bridge of his nose. He did not look forward to looking at page after page of numbers. What's worse, he wasn't sure he was up to the task of finding anything in that mess of numbers. Nick pulled out his coffeepot and dusted off his printer. While his coffee brewed, he printed. Then taking a sip of coffee, he began the search.

By Sunday night, Nick was exhausted. His eyes watered and could barely focus. His head and back ached from sitting and staring at sheet after sheet of paper. Despite his pains, he was satisfied with his work.

He found there were two copies of the accounting records. The first was from two weeks prior to Wood's disappearance, July 2. The second copy was from July 16. By comparing the two, Nick found a 50 percent increase in transactions from the July 2 to the July 16 report. For every two deposits in the July 2 copy, there now existed a third transaction, a transfer of funds, in the July 16 copy. This transfer was a small percentage of the previous two deposits. Interestingly, the total funds in the accounts sync up until July 7. The money never left the charity accounts. It was just transferred to a new budget line item. Except on July 7 and again on July 9 and 10, the phantom budget items were transferred to several different bank accounts registered in the Caymans and Switzerland.

This proved nothing, Nick knew, as the accountant could easily have been maneuvering this money and hiding it, especially with the help of the treasurer. Since the funds never left, at least not until July 7, they would just have needed to submit reports that omitted the phantom budget items, a report like the one from July 2. If, as the police would, one assumed the suspects were guilty, this would be the smoking gun evidence. If one assumed they were innocent, a timetable for when the real perpetrators accessed the Little Drummer Boy computer system, inserted fraudulent data, took the money, and left the accountant and treasurer on the hook emerged. If one had this information and the laptop that never received the new data…well, that would prove the money was moved recently and would likely exonerate Wood and Dash. It certainly wouldn't hurt their case.

So why didn't Wood go to the police? Nick thought this possible dirty cop theory could be the answer. If Wood figured out a cop was after him, he'd likely not know who to trust, at least until he figured out who set him up. He would then need someone he could trust to get the evidence where it would do him good.

*****

Monday morning, Nick was out the door early. Having a timeline of July 2 to the 7, Nick was able to pull up the Little Drummer Boy staff schedules from the files Wood left. From those schedules, he determined a list of people in the office who could have gained access to the system.

Two people were out of the office—Wood and Dash. Wood took a two-week vacation which explained his laptop's lack of updates. Dash, who was a board member, didn't come to the offices at all during this time. The offices were closed on July 4 and 5 for Independence Day. This narrowed the search to people with access on July 3 or July 6.

Given that holiday staffing was light, the receptionist, Nora Holbrook, and an intern, Robyn Goode, were the only two present both days. From what he could tell, Robyn started in mid-June and worked five days a week. Her schedule bounced between accounting, PR, and volunteer services. Nick had little else on the intern besides her name, so he decided to pay a visit to Mrs. Holbrook first.

The main office of the Little Drummer Boy was located at 12 Tower Way. This twenty-story office building and attached garage housed a number of different businesses. The building was secure, requiring a key card to access and operate the elevator or an escort by a security officer. At night, the building was accessible to any key card holder, but there was no on-site security. Cameras were monitored remotely by the security company. Nick got all this information from Glen, the affable security officer escorting Nick to the eighth floor, where the Little Drummer Boy office occupied half the building's footprint.

Nick thanked Glen and shook his hand as he exited the elevator. He was greeted by Nora Holbrook as he entered the reception area.

"Good morning! Welcome to the Little Drummer Boy, Mr.?"

"Saint, Nick Saint."

"Welcome, Mr. Saint."

"Thanks. Are you Nora Holbrook?" Nick asked.

"Yes, yes, I am. Do we know each other?" Nora asked, a quizzical expression on her face. Her body language was tense, off put by this stranger looking for her, especially after what happened to Morgan.

"Not that I know of, ma'am," Nick answered. He held his hand out, offering a business card. Nora took it from him.

"A private investigator?"

"Yes, and I was hoping I could ask you about the missing money."

Nora sank into her chair. "Look, I can't help you. The police have told me not to discuss the case with anyone but them. And now, with Morgan murdered...," Nora trailed off.

"Nora," Nick said, "I can respect not wanting to ignore the police orders. I can understand being afraid after a coworker was murdered, so if you ask me to leave, I will. I'll just ask that you answer one question before you decide if you'll speak with me."

"Go ahead," Nora said. "One question, and then you're gone. Okay?"

"Okay," Nick replied. "Where's your computer?"

Nora laughed. "My computer? I don't have one. I'm a volunteer receptionist. I retired from hairdressing, oh, almost ten years ago. When my Bernie died a few years back, I was lonely. I did some work here, packing fliers to be mailed out, wrapping gifts for the kids, and, well, one thing led to another. I greet people like at Walmart but much less soul draining."

It was Nick's turn to laugh. "So you don't have access to a computer at all?"

"Mr. Saint, I'm pushing eighty. I don't need email or anything else from a computer, at least not here." She picked up her book. "I read. I talk." Nora pulled out her cell phone. "And I check Facebook to keep up with the grandkids."

Nick thanked her and headed for the door. "Can I ask you one last question?" he asked.

Nora thought for a minute then said, "Sure, why not."

"What do you know about Robyn Goode?"

"Oh, that little thing? She's a sweet girl. Twenty years old, I think. Said she was getting college credit for interning. She was a sophomore, or was it a junior? I think it was sophomore. Anyway, she's in business school, but I'm not sure it was for her. She was a hard worker, and she always brought doughnuts and coffee on Friday. I insisted she take money but she never would. I asked her how she could afford it, you know, being an unpaid intern and college student. She would just laugh and say her parents were contributing to her education."

"You wouldn't happen to remember where she got the doughnuts, would you?"

"Some mom-and-pop shop. It had a funny name. What was it...hmmmm...the Hole Story, I think. Something like that. It was a pun about doughnuts and bagels."

"You wouldn't happen to have a picture of her, would you?"

"Who, Robyn? No, I can't figure this camera phone out to save my life. My grandkids take pictures of everything with it. But me? No way. And Robyn, bless her, doesn't use social media. Can you believe it? Maybe there's hope for her generation yet."

Nick thanked Nora for her time and took the elevator to the lobby.

"Glen!" Nick called to the security officer behind the front desk. "I need a favor."

It took some convincing, but Glen finally gave in and checked the security records for Robyn Goode. He found a headshot from her ID. Unfortunately, he couldn't print it out, but Nick was able to take a snapshot on his phone before he left.

Sitting in his car, Nick pulled out a small notebook from his pocket. Under Sandra Wescot, he wrote, "Glen—opera tickets for wife." Nick hated trading gifts for favors, but sometimes, he did what he had to do.

The Hole Story—a bagel and doughnut experience—was located in a former industrial area that had been revitalized as the cultural hub for the millennial hipster. There were boutique shops specializing in bow ties and mustache wax, coffee bars that roasted their own beans on-site and frowned upon anyone who put cream or sugar into their drink, restaurants that specialized in "deconstructed food" (a term Nick never could wrap his head around), art galleries featuring local artists who often lived above in small poorly ventilated but excellently lit apartments, and bars with trendy themes such as the 1980s or pinball. It was all very trendy, very niche, and very much not something Nick understood. Having lived through the 1980s, he wasn't sure why anyone was nostalgic for it, at least in a going-out-to-the-bar sense. The social scene of the '80s was different, to say the least. He liked the movies though; it was a golden age of comedy, in his opinion.

"Hi, can I get a chocolate glaze and a large black coffee?" Nick asked when he made it to the front of the queue at the Hole Story.

"Sure, anything else?"

Nick pulled out his phone. "Yeah, do you know this girl? She goes by Robyn Goode?"

"That'll be $4.25 for your order, and, no, I don't think I know her."

Nick handed the woman behind the counter a fifty and told her to keep the change.

She took the money and said, "Let me see the picture again." She looked closely this time and called out, "Tim! Tim, come over here."

A man in his midthirties, his apron covered in flour, long hair and beard in a sanitary hairnet, came out from the back. "What's up?"

"This guy is looking for a girl named Robyn something."

"Goode, Robyn Goode," Nick interjected.

"Yeah, Robyn Goode. She kind of looks like Faith, right?"

Nick showed the picture on his phone to Tim.

"Yeah, I think that is her. A dozen doughnuts and a ten-cup coffee box every Friday. Haven't seen her in a while though."

"And you said her name was Faith? Any chance you got a last name?"

"No, we just get a first name for the order."

After eating what was a truly exceptional doughnut, Nick began to canvass the neighborhood in search of Faith. Sipping his coffee, which compared to the pastry was disappointing at best, Nick went down the block. He stopped in every shop, restaurant, and bar that was open.

One nice thing about this neighborhood is that most of these businesses are not chains and locally owned, Nick thought. *The staff is small, often owner operated, and they know their customers.*

Unfortunately, no one else seemed to know Faith, at least not in the heart of the district. It was an unseasonably warm day, so Nick ditched his coat in his car and headed to the north end of town, checking out the shops and bars along the way. The number of storefronts dwindled and the number of boarded-up buildings grew the farther north he went. Gentrification had not yet reached this end of town, at least not as fully as just a few blocks south. Here and there, an upcycling vintage clothing store or an alternative hairstyling experience had opened. A few surviving dive bars were open too. Their crowd was rougher and older. The bars were holdovers from the postindustrial, premillennial hipster eras. These patrons were those who had yet to sell off their aging homes and business to real estate developers, hoping that, as the rolling tide of progress got closer, they'd get better offers.

To Nick's surprise, he came upon a Catholic church. A once-grand building, its stone walls and towering spires were now blackened by a hundred years of soot. The landscaping was in need of attention, and the doors and window frames could use a new coat of paint. Nick read the plaque on the wall, "St. Matthias Church, established 1890. Lord, you know everyone's heart, Acts 1:24."

From behind him, Nick heard footsteps approaching. He turned to see an old man dressed for colder weather. He looked tired and dirty. Nick took him to be homeless.

"The AA meeting doesn't start until three," the old man said.

"Oh, I'm not here for that," Nick said. "I'm looking for Faith."

Nick reached into his pocket for his phone to show the man her picture when he heard a voice call out from the door of the church, "Aren't we all, my friend?"

Nick turned to the door and saw a young priest, maybe thirty years old, waving the old man inside. "The meeting doesn't start for an hour, but I usually set the coffee out a little early," the priest said. "Could you use a refill?" He motioned to the half-empty cup in Nick's hand. The coffee had gone cold a while ago.

In the basement of the church, there were ten chairs in a circle and an urn of coffee on a folding table. Roger, the old man, was seated in one of the chairs, sipping coffee from a small Styrofoam cup.

"So, my friend, you're in search of faith?" The priest motioned for Nick to take a seat.

Nick pulled his phone out from his pocket. "I am, but capital F, Faith. Do you know her?"

It was obvious that the priest recognized her, but he said nothing. "I'm sorry, I can't help you, Mr.?"

"Saint, Nick Saint."

"Mr. Saint, but I've helped many others find a different kind of faith. Perhaps I could help you with that instead?"

Nick paused to sip his coffee. Considering the price, this cup was much better than his last. "Sorry, Father, but I'm not part of your flock. I wouldn't want to take up your time. Thanks for the coffee."

Nick turned to leave, but the priest continued speaking, "Consider it a gift, Mr. Saint."

Nick replied, "The giver of every good and perfect gift has called upon us to mimic God's giving by grace and through faith, and this is not of ourselves."

"Very clever, Nick Saint, quoting Saint Nicholas. I prefer 'Patience with others is love. Patience with self is hope. Patience with God is faith.'"

The priest then excused himself to greet others arriving early for the meeting. "Patience with God is faith…" Nick turned this around in his mind for a minute, then he pulled up a chair.

About halfway through the meeting, Nick started to think he had made a mistake when he heard the door to the basement open. He looked up and saw Faith. She apologized quietly to the priest, who placed his hand on her shoulder and quietly assured her that it was okay and asked her to join the group.

Nick had never been to an AA meeting before, but it was very much like TV—coffee, doughnuts, anyone interested in speaking taking their turn to tell their story. Some of the stories were very sad, and some were funny. Some were inspirational and hopeful. The story he was here for, Faith's, never came. She sat and listened but never spoke.

After the meeting, she waited for the crowd to thin. She took the priest aside, and they spoke for a few minutes, and then he left.

Nick approached Faith and introduced himself, "Faith? I'm Nick, Nick Saint. I'm a private investigator working for Stephen Dash. Do you have a minute to talk?"

Faith angrily pushed Nick away. "No, I don't have time to talk. I don't know who that is. I've never heard of him." She started to walk away, and Nick followed her.

He tried again. "If you're not familiar with Stephen Dash, what can you tell me about the Little Drummer Boy?"

"Never heard of it," she said, still walking toward the exit.

Nick pulled up a picture up on his phone. This was not the close-up of Faith's face that he had been showing around town but the full shot of Robyn Goode's ID badge. "This is you, isn't it, Faith? Or should I call you Robyn?"

Faith stopped and turned to face Nick. In a hushed tone, she said, "Put that away. Please?"

Nick looked into her eyes, noticing the telltale shimmer of tears forming. "But this is you, isn't it, Faith?" Nick asked, his piercing stare holding her gaze.

Finally, Faith broke, her eyes turning down and away from Nick. "You don't understand. I had no choice."

"What do you mean you had no choice?" Nick asked.

Faith looked around the room. A few stragglers remained by the coffee, but they were more interested in getting a cup to-go than anything being said by her or Nick.

"Look," Faith said, "I'm in a bad way. I've made mistakes, lots of them, but I swear I didn't steal any money from the charity."

"But you did help whoever did," Nick said.

"You're right, I 'helped,'" she intoned sarcastically. "I was forced to do it."

"Didn't the police ever come to you?" Nick asked.

"Why would they? I was a summer intern with barely any access to the computer system. I was able to check email, type Word documents, but I didn't have access to anything sensitive. They had their suspects, and I was able to just disappear."

"How did you do it then? What did they need from someone with low-level access to the system? And why go through the trouble of setting you up with a fake identity to get them no access whatsoever? They could've gotten better access so much easier from the outside. I doubt they had robust security. I'm sure a decent hacker—"

Faith cut him off, "A hack from the outside would be harder to cover up, or so they told me when I asked the same thing. I don't know much about computers. I just did what they told me to do."

"Okay then, so what did you do?" Nick asked.

"I could access the computers from an inside terminal. I was given a thumb drive, a log-in, and a password. I show up, log in, plug it in, drag and drop a file, open it, pull the drive, and log out. Whatever was in that program did the rest."

Nick thought for a moment, and Faith started for the door once again. "Why did you do it? Who made you do it?"

"Look, I told you, I've made mistakes." Faith's voice cracked as she tried to hold back the tears. "I was scared and alone. He offered me hope. And once I'd told him my secrets...once I opened up to him thinking he could help me...they used me. Do what they said or risk losing everything."

She wiped a tear from her face. "And then the next thing I know, Mr. Wood is missing. The treasurer is being investigated, and money is missing," she trailed off.

"Why not go to the police?" Nick asked.

"He owns cops like he owns me. And if I turn myself in? I just look like another accomplice. No one will believe me. I have no proof. I took a job at a children's charity under an assumed name. The only thing I'll do is incriminate myself for more crimes."

"Whatever they have on you, it can't be worse than this," Nick said, hoping that it was the truth.

Faith broke down. Through her sobs, she yelled, "You don't know that! You know nothing! They'll take my son! They won't k me. They'll just send me to hell!"

She covered her face and cried into her hands. "I wish they'd kill me like Wood…but they won't. If I keep my head down…maybe, just maybe, I'll just get to stay here, in purgatory."

"Faith, I can help you. Tell me who is doing this," Nick implored.

"No one can help me now, Mr. Saint." She turned, wiping her eyes with her sleeve, and ran for the exit.

Nick looked around, thankful that the only person left in the room was the priest. "Do you know her story?"

The priest nodded. "Unfortunately, it was told to me under the veil of the confessional. I can't tell you much, but she is a troubled woman who got in a bad way. She's trying to make amends, but… she needs help, Mr. Saint. I can pray for her and ask for the blessings of God upon her, but you—"

"I can help," Nick said.

"Yes, you can," the priest said. "Are you going to the police?"

"Not yet. She's right. It won't help my client and will just make trouble for her." Nick handed his card to the priest. "Give this to her, please?"

"Gladly. Can I do anything else for you, Mr. Saint?"

"Yeah, does Faith have a last name?"

"It's Garza. Go with God, my friend."

Chapter 11

The next day, Nick looked through all the public records he could. Faith Garza was not a common name, but it wasn't one of a kind either. Eventually, he found the right Faith Garza. She was older than Nick had assumed. At thirty-three, she easily passed for twenty. Faith had her first brush with the law when she was twenty. She was expelled from university for violating their ethics policy when she was caught selling exams. She had somehow obtained a few copies of a particularly hard chemistry exam and was making a tidy sum selling it. Her clients fared no better though only those caught red-handed were expelled. Faith, it seemed, never turned in the rest of her clients even when offered academic suspension in lieu of expulsion.

After her expulsion, Faith fell in with a bad crowd and got addicted to painkillers, then moved to heroin, a cheaper high, when she ran out of money. As money grew tight, she began to hustle, stealing and pawning what she could. Fortunately, for Faith, when she was caught pawning a stolen laptop, it was her father's. He pleaded with the judge for rehabilitation rather than jail. She was sentenced to six months' probation and rehab.

Faith's public record then picked up a few years later. Now twenty-five, she was arrested for possession of narcotics, driving under the influence, and resisting arrest. She served two years of a four-year prison sentence. At twenty-seven, she had a baby, a boy. There was no mention of the father, but the timing of the pregnancy was suspicious given her likely incarceration at the time of conception. She got a job as a waitress and eventually started tending bar. She remained clean until six months ago when she was arrested for multiple charges: driving under the influence, reckless endangerment, destruction of property, failure to follow traffic signals, and possession of narcotics with the intent to distribute.

On the night of her arrest, there were multiple early morning calls to 911 about a possible drunk driver that was swerving down the road, striking parked cars, striking mailboxes, and running multiple stop signs. The police responded to the area and followed a trail of destruction to a car parked in the yard of Faith Garza. The vehicle was still running, driver's door open, and the keys still in the ignition. The vehicle's sole occupant was the owner, Faith Garza. She was found passed out and unarousable in the passenger seat. EMS was called, and she was taken to the local emergency department for evaluation. A search of the vehicle found a bag of pills, later determined to be oxycodone, underneath the driver's seat. The number of pills suggested an intent to sell rather than recreational use.

At the emergency room, Faith was found to have a blood alcohol level below the legal limit to drive but also the presence of opiates in her urine. She was observed until sober and released into the custody of the police. Her medical record was subpoenaed for the blood alcohol level and the drug screen. A court filing showed that Faith's defense attorney had questioned evidence in the case and was working to have it thrown out of court. His argument was that there was no legal chain of custody for the blood and urine samples and should not be admissible as evidence. He further argued that the drugs found in the car should be inadmissible as they had no right to search the vehicle as they did not first use a drug dog to sniff. He was arguing that they executed an unlawful search of the vehicle without probable cause. He was requesting that the charges of driving under the influence be reduced to reckless driving and failure to follow traffic control signs and all other charges be dismissed.

Nick was unsure if any of those arguments would stick. What he did know was that her attorney was able to make enough of an argument to tie things up in court for a few months. Faith was remanded to house arrest with allowances to leave for her AA meetings and to work. She lost her job at the bar and was now bagging groceries just down the street from her house. Her son was in the custody of her mother with no visitation rights until after her trial. Now Nick knew Faith's story, but he still didn't know who forced her into the Little Drummer Boy plot. Faith had said he had cops just like he had her and that she told him her secrets. Who would you tell your secrets to besides your priest? Your lawyer?

Nick checked the name of the lawyer representing Faith, Albert Zane. A Web search only brought up one Albert Zane, JD. He was a partner at a corporate law practice. "A corporate lawyer? Practicing criminal law?" Nick thought aloud. He tried to look up other cases, but he couldn't filter by defense attorney in the court records. He opened the site of Rich and Wellhoff, Partners in Law. He found the biography section and pulled up partner Albert Zane.

"Acting CEO of Rich and Wellhoff, Mr. Zane graduated from Stanford Law, class of 1994. He served as a public defender until 2000. He joined Rich and Wellhoff and became a junior partner in 2010. He became a senior partner in 2017. Following the death of Stanley Wellhoff, Mr. Zane was promoted to interim CEO. He provides pro bono defense representation in a limited capacity and is a member of the local rotary club..."

Nick stopped reading. *This guy has got to be worth a decent amount of money. Why steal from a charity that, as far as I can tell, has no connection to Zane or Rich and Wellhoff? And why frame Dash and Wood for it?* Nick thought. An Internet search for Zane came up with a few dozen articles in local papers and academic journals. From an interview a few years ago, Nick read that Zane loved his work as a public defender, helping those that needed it most, providing a constitutionally protected right to the citizens of his city. However, the caseloads were large. He often worked long hours, and he felt he was defending the wrong people, guilty people. He needed a change, and he had a chance encounter with an old college friend who helped him start his journey into corporate law.

When golf and squash at the club failed to excite him, he found his mind wandering back into the courtroom. He decided to return to criminal defense law part-time and pro bono. He would defend those that needed him the most. He particularly liked taking cases where he felt police officers were being wrongfully accused and where he felt the police overstepped or made a mistake.

"If we, as a society, are to trust the police and they us, we need to ensure proper justice on both sides of the blue line," Zane was quoted as having said. In the last five years, he handled the cases of half a dozen cops and a handful of other cases, including Faith's. Faith's case made the news twice, once when she was arrested. She was found passed out in the front seat of her car, keys still in the ignition. The car was damaged with blood and hair on the passenger side mirror. A pedestrian, who lay dying in the ICU from a hit-and-run accident, was found to have been struck by the mirror from Faith's car and had then fallen under the wheels. The second time was when she was released to house arrest with allowances to go to work, AA meetings, and scheduled visits with her son. Her lawyer convinced the judge that there were procedural problems with the police handling the investigation. He also portrayed Faith in a good enough light that she was saved from pretrial incarceration. The trial had been delayed several times as Zane fought to get charges and evidence dismissed and generally slowed down the process as much as he could.

Zane's work in the corporate world was much less newsworthy except for the Rich and Wellhoff acquisition of a large new account last year: the corporate and familial interest of the Honor family. The Honors were currently fourth-generation bakers although it had been at least two generations since a hand had touched flour in the family.

Gabriel Honore arrived in the United States on a boat from France. He passed through Ellis Island in 1920 at the age of twenty. His mother and father had both died quite young, and Gabriel, one of six children and the second oldest, had to find work. He apprenticed to a baker and became quite adept at bread making and was learning the art of pastry. When he was fifteen, war came to France. His family was displaced, his town all but destroyed. The baker to whom he apprenticed joined the fight. Gabriel did not hear from him again. With his siblings starving and essentially homeless, Gabriel knew he had to take action. He lied about his age and joined the army. He sent his pay home to his siblings. His older sister, Mary, used the money to raise the younger children.

Gabriel, discharged from the army, was determined to make a better life for his family. What he found upon his return devastated him. Three of the youngest had died of disease. His older sister, traumatized by the loss, had run off and was never heard from again. His brother, one year his junior, had joined the army as well and was killed in action.

Gabriel looked across the ocean to America where he hoped to start fresh. He eventually settled and, after working for a number of years as a laborer, was able to start a small bakery. Wanting to sound more American, he changed his last name to Honor and insisted on being called Gabe. Though he had a fine assortment of baked goods, he became renowned for his cookies. Christmas was the busiest and best time for Gabe. He married and had a son, Michael. Michael learned from his father, and together, Honor and Son became the place to go for cookies, cakes, and pies locally.

Gabriel retired in 1965, leaving the business in the hands of his son, Michael. Michael changed the name to Honor and Sons. He had two, Gabriel and Michael Jr. Honor and Sons continued to grow. Gabriel and Michael Jr. both enjoyed the cookie business but had different passions. Gabriel, like his namesake grandfather, learned and loved to bake. Michael Jr. was interested in the business of selling. When he graduated from college in 1969, Honor and Sons had five locations and still couldn't keep up with the demand. Michael Jr. avoided the draft due to a heart condition, but his brother, Gabriel, was not so lucky. He was sent to Vietnam and never returned home.

Michael Jr. became the successor to his father and inherited the Honor and Sons bakeries. He took the company from bakery to factory, launching a regional, then national line of cookies by 1983. His father continued to operate the five bakeries until his untimely death at the age of sixty in 1987. Michael Jr. closed all but one of the bakeries, preserving the original shop opened by his grandfather as a retail outlet for his factory products.

Michael Jr. had a son, Joseph, in 1984 and daughter, Sarah, in 1987, with his wife, June. He rebranded in 1994 under the name

Honor Family Cookies. Honor Family Cookies became an international product. Michael Jr. began expanding into other markets, primarily to vertically integrate his supply chain by taking control of wheat processing and sugar refining. Other investments were to diversify the company portfolio and included property, golf resorts, and restaurants. Honor Family Cookies were rolled into his investment company, Gabriel Industries.

Sarah, a gifted musician, went into the theater, and naturally, Honor Family Cookies sponsored her shows. Joseph, like his father, attended business school and then joined Gabriel Industries. In 2017, Michael Jr. fell ill and passed away in February 2018. Joseph was named as successor to Michael Jr. He and his sister split the family's large estate. Their mother, though living, had suffered a stroke a number of years earlier, and the children served as her conservators.

The law offices of Thomas and Yves had represented Michael Jr. and his business interests for decades. However, when Michael Jr. fell ill, Joseph filled in for his father as acting CEO. During that time, Thomas and Yves were replaced by Rich and Wellhoff. They provided legal counsel for both the Honor family and Gabriel Industries. Albert Zane was named as the lead counsel for Gabriel Industries, nominated by the Gabriel Industries board of directors. This multi-billion-dollar client likely cemented Albert Zane's ascendency to the head of Rich and Wellhoff upon Mr. Wellhoff's death.

As far as Nick could tell, Albert Zane was a stand-up citizen. He was successful and, with his success, gave back to the community. Nick was worried this was a dead end, but who else could hold sway over Faith? Who else would know her secrets?

Chapter 12

Stephen Dash had not had a good night's sleep in weeks. As the audit progressed, he became increasingly aware that something was terribly amiss. First was the cryptic voicemail from Wood. Then Wood disappeared. The auditors began asking for very particular documents that Stephen knew could only mean trouble. When it became apparent that money was missing—a lot of money—Stephen could hardly sleep. He tossed and turned so much, Holly sent him to the couch. Then he was sent to jail. He was there for a few days, only but the anxiety, constant noise, and fear—it was all too much.

When he was released, it was to a home that was never his. The sale of their old home had concluded just before his arrest. The movers had just finished packing their trucks when the police took them to examine for evidence. His old home now belonged to a new family. His new home was empty and uninviting. He did have his bed and a few items that the police had left, some clothes and personal items. He also had a new couch, which was nice. Holly's story about a private investigator that may or may not be Santa Claus still didn't make any sense, especially the bit about how the couch was delivered, almost as if by magic. But, he figured, sleep deprivation could do crazy things to your mind. He had hoped after a good night's sleep, he would be able to clear some things up.

He felt lucky to have his own bed again and, more importantly, a private bathroom. The prospect of twenty years of doing his private business in the open was just one of the many fears he had about the very real possibility of going to prison. The first nights at home,

Stephen was beyond exhausted but still he could not sleep. He tossed and turned and went to the couch. Staring at the starry night sky through the windows, he lay awake, wishing he knew what was going to happen.

The Tuesday night following his release from jail, he tried a combination of vigorous exercise, calming tea, and guided meditation courtesy of an app on Holly's phone. She had found it useful in holding it together given everything that had been going on. Stephen finally fell into a deep and well-deserved rest.

The next morning would have been one to sleep late, and Stephen was definitely tired enough to stay in bed most of the day. Unfortunately, for both Holly, who also hadn't been sleeping well, and Stephen, they were awakened at six thirty in the morning by a rapping at the door, followed by a fairly urgent and repeated ringing of the doorbell.

Stephen rose, pulled on a bathrobe over his pajamas, and put on a pair of slippers. These were plush and comfortable but still reminded him of the jail-issued shoes he had been forced to wear during his brief stay. Having been woken so abruptly from his first good sleep in a while, he reflexively started to say, "Someone had better be dead or dying," which was something he used to say when he was disturbed after business hours by his office. Then he remembered Morgan Wood and thought better of it. Instead, he said, "Someone is at the door."

Holly, still half asleep, having never been a morning person during the best of times, gave him a look that was a mixture of incredulity at the obviousness of the statement and fear at the implication. She, too, had been thinking of Morgan Wood.

"Maybe we should call the police?" Holly asked. "I mean, who knows about our new house? Who do we know that would visit this early and unannounced?"

Stephen thought for a moment, looked down at his ankle and the attached monitor, and said, "I've had enough of the police this month. I'm going to answer the door."

Holly dressed quickly, pulling sweatpants and a sweatshirt over her nightclothes. She grabbed tennis shoes and pulled them on quickly and found her cell phone as the front door opened. She heard a familiar voice echoing through the empty house. "Nick Saint, private investigator."

Stephen led Nick into the kitchen. Nick sat a bag down on the counter. "Have you eaten?" he asked.

"No, we haven't eaten. I was, until moments ago, sleeping. Do you know what time it is?"

"It's early. That's why I asked if you had eaten." Nick pulled bagels, cream cheese, plates, plastic utensils, coffee, tea, muffins, fruit, butter, jam, cream, and sugar from the bag.

"Good morning, Nick! Can I assume your early and unannounced visit means you have good news?" Holly picked up a tea.

"No news, good or bad, but I do have questions."

"So you're the detective that thinks he's Santa Claus. I know my wife hired you, but I'm not so sure I want a crazy person poking around my case. I'm in enough trouble as it is. If the DA thinks I'm sending someone out to harass witnesses, well, I don't know. It wouldn't help me, I know that for sure. Also, I'd like to point out we cannot pay you. All our assets are frozen."

"First," Nick began, "I never claimed to be Santa Claus." He looked at Stephen coolly and continued, "When you are cleared of the charges, I assume you'll have the means to pay me my fees. And as for witness intimidation? If I'm reading the situation correctly, the police aren't looking too deeply into this, and they don't have many witnesses for me to intimidate. The books show money being moved around internally for a while before suddenly being moved out of the country. Wood was seen as an accomplice, and now he's dead. So you're it. Anyone I talk to is likely not even on the police radar."

"And who might you talk to, Nick?" Stephen asked.

"To start with, Faith Garza."

Holly and Stephen looked at each other and both shrugged as if to say, "No one I know." Stephen turned back to Nick. "And who is Faith Garza?"

Nick sipped his coffee. "She's also known as Robyn Goode."

"I know that name. Why do I know that name?" Stephen palmed his forehead and scratched his scalp with his fingers. "It's too early for this shit, Nick. I'm tired. I haven't had any coffee. And you ambush me in my pajamas to play games with me? Just tell me what you know."

Nick pushed a coffee cup to Stephen. "I know it's early. That's why I brought coffee: one Splenda, one sugar, two pumps hazelnut."

Stephen stared at Nick as he described his preferred coffee, then he looked at Holly. "Told you," was all she said.

"Eat. Get dressed. I'll wait." Nick took his coffee and sat on the couch to watch the sunrise.

An hour later, fed, showered, and dressed, Stephen and Holly joined Nick in the great room. Nick pulled in a stool from the kitchen. He had the Dashes sit on the couch and he opposite them on the stool. "So Robyn Goode, you remember her yet?" Nick asked.

Stephen shook his head no. Nick pulled her picture out, and Stephen's eyes brightened. "The intern, the college kid, right?"

"Did you know her well?" Nick asked.

"No. I only met her once or twice. I met Morgan for lunch and to get the June quarterly report. She was packing envelopes or something. I don't remember much else."

"And you don't know the name Faith Garza?" Nick asked.

"No, never heard of her until you mentioned her this morning. You said she is Robyn Goode?"

"Correct. Faith is a thirty-three-year-old serial offender. She has a history of drug and alcohol abuse. Recently, she was arrested on some more serious charges."

"Wait, no, that can't be right. There's some sort of mistake. We work with kids. We background every employee, including interns," Stephen said.

"Well, yeah, the mistake is the Little Drummer Boy had a criminal as an intern working under an assumed identity," Nick replied.

"What was she doing there, Nick? Is she responsible for stealing the money?" Stephen asked.

"I'm still working on that," Nick said. He took a pause before continuing, "But I know she wasn't working alone. I think she's a pawn in whatever is going on here."

"So take her to the police," Stephen said. "Get them to make her talk."

"Stephen, haven't you had enough of the police for a while? At best, they'll just make her out to be your accomplice."

"I don't understand," Holly said. "Why would that be?"

"She's a waitress and bartender with a drug problem and no computer skills. There's no evidence that there was any hacking or tampering with the files, and she somehow got a fake name around the Little Drummer Boy background check. Unless she tells them who she's really working for, they'll pin her as working with someone on the inside, someone like you or Wood. And I think she's more afraid of whoever she's working for than she is of the police."

"I'm totally fucked, aren't I?" Stephen asked.

"Not totally, just mostly." After a long pause, Nick asked, "Where did you get the money for this house?"

"It was my money. It was legal. Thank you very much for asking."

"That much is obvious. The money didn't leave the Little Drummer Boy accounts until July. You've had your money since at least the time you were married, right? Your golden years' nest egg, correct?"

"Yeah, it was. How did you know about the wire transfers in July? That...that wasn't public information."

"I have my sources. So where did you get the money?"

"Trust him, Stephen. He believes you. He wants to help." Holly laid a hand on Stephen's shoulder.

"It's a trust fund. And, no, I'm not some rich kid with a trust fund. This is the first time I've touched the money. See, I never knew my father. He died before I was born. He had a life insurance policy. My mom put the money in a trust for me. She had a good job and thought the money would be better off being saved for me. She was the trustee until I turned twenty-five. She put some of it in bonds and stable investments and took a portion to invest in the stock market. She picked a few winners, Apple, Microsoft, Google, to name a few. All in all, I had about ten million when I took over. I converted it all into bonds, CDs, savings accounts. I figured that I had enough money for one man. No need to get greedy. And with a moderate return, the interest on ten million is pretty good."

"And you told Holly you wanted to see the world when you retire?" Nick asked.

"I did. When I retire, I want us to enjoy our lives."

"Does anybody else know about this money or this plan?"

"No, not really. I don't advertise that I have money. I'm not ashamed of it or anything, but it's not like I earned it. It was a windfall from an otherwise tragic event."

"Have you ever spent any of it before you bought this house?"

"Not a dime."

"So about the time money starts to get moved around the Little Drummer Boy account, you start spending big from your trust?" Nick asked.

"Yes, that is one of the stronger points against me, I admit."

"So why did you start spending the money?"

"After my mom died, I started thinking about her and my father. I was close with my mom's family, but I was never told anything about my father's family. I'd thought about it before, but I had a good life, and I just decided to let it go. But the death of a loved one—it makes you think. So I took one of those HeritageDNA tests."

"Did you find anything interesting?" Nick asked.

"At first, no. I'm English on my mother's side—I knew that already—and a mix of French and Irish, I assume on my father's side. There were a few cousins I'd never heard of from my mother's side but nothing significant."

"And that's why you spent your money? You have some distant cousins you have never heard of?"

"No, no, I got a call a few weeks after I got my DNA test results back. You can keep your results private so other biological matches can't see you so you don't have a bunch of distant relatives knocking on your door, I guess. Anyway, you can still see if a public profile matches you, even if you have your account set as private."

"Who called you, Stephen?" Nick slid to the edge of his seat.

"My father or someone claiming to be my father. I now know it was more than just a claim. It was the truth."

"I thought your father died?"

"So did I," Stephen said. "He didn't though. He was married and had an affair with my mother. The life insurance? Hush money. He signed away all parental rights in exchange for the money and the promise that my mother would never reveal who my father was. My mother took that secret to the grave."

"And who is your father?"

"Was Nick. Was. My father was Michael Honor Jr."

Chapter 13

"Michael Honor Jr. is your father?" Nick asked.

"Yes, the recently deceased king of a cookie empire was my father."

Nick put up his hands in front of his chest and rolled them around, signaling for Stephen to keep going.

"It was the summer of 2016 when I got the first call. It wasn't actually Michael. It was his office. I think he knew that calling himself would've been a mistake because anyone getting a cold call from a billionaire claiming to be his estranged and presumed dead father could reasonably call bullshit and hang up. It would be a lot like that Kenyan prince email scam. Nobody would buy it. But the offices of a wealthy businessman calling a tax attorney asking for a lunch meeting? Well, not unusual. We usually court these big clients, not the other way around, but it's not entirely unreasonable. I was actually reluctant to go at first. My plate was already full, so to speak, and a cold-call lunch was not really in my time budget. But setting the meetup at one of the best steak houses in the city, well, how often can you have lunch with a billionaire? And my firm is small but well regarded, and a big client wouldn't hurt the firm any.

"I took the offer. Now I wasn't expecting Michael to show. I assumed it would be his legal team or his business manager, maybe the COO, the accounting team, or some combination of any of the above coming to pick my brain and offer a contract for some work.

"When I arrived, I immediately knew something was up. It was noon on Friday at a very well-known and very expensive downtown restaurant. It should've been full or at least very busy. It was empty. No one at the bar. No one queued at the maître d'. No one at any tables. I was greeted immediately and taken to a table where Michael Honor Jr. was seated. By himself. He stood with an almost wide-eyed stare. His eyes glazed over a bit, and I thought he might cry. It was possibly the most deeply uncomfortable I've ever felt and that included the sex talk my date's mother and father gave me before prom in the twelfth grade. Try pinning a corsage while a grown man and woman talk about their daughter's other flower.

"Anyway, he shook my hand firmly for an uncomfortably long time. We're seated and offered a wine list. He declined and ordered a bottle that likely cost more than this couch, and he ordered other drinks too. Now I'm not one to drink much, especially not at a lunch meeting, but I felt I was going to that afternoon, so I canceled all my meetings through my administrative assistant. Have I mentioned how uncomfortable this was? We sat in silence for a few minutes until the wine arrived. After a lengthy and very artful decanting, we were served an excellent wine, which, if I'm being honest, tasted like the fifteen-dollar bottle of red that we had last night. That's when Michael asked me a question I was totally unprepared for. He asked me to tell him about my father. Well, not much to tell, I said. He died before I was born. Mom didn't talk about him. I never met his family. He asked if my mother ever remarried, and I told him no. He asked if I knew why, and I told him the only thing I could, which was I assumed she loved him until the end. At this, he actually did cry. I considered leaving at this point because despite the expensive yet indistinguishable cheap wine, this lunch was going very…strangely.

"When he composed himself, he looked me straight in the eyes. He said, 'Son, your father didn't die before or after your birth. He's sitting right here.' I actually don't remember saying it, but he told me I stammered something unintelligible and then told him to fuck off. He slid a folder across the table, and I opened it. Inside was a photo of my mother and him and a birth certificate with him listed as the father. Now I have my birth certificate, and there is no father listed, but this looked like a real birth certificate. It even had the raised seal of the state like mine.

"So I asked him, 'If you're my father, why contact me now?' And he told me that he tried to find me a long time ago, that my mother must've changed her name. I checked the birth certificate again, Margaret Keene. Keene is my mom's maiden name, but I always knew her as Angela Dash.

"He told me that he met my mother, then Margaret Keene, in 1974. She was twenty-four years old and had taken a job as his assistant. The mid to late 1970s were a busy and chaotic time for him. He had married his college sweetheart in 1971, a woman whom he loved very much. However, taking his family business from a few stores to a national brand in under fifteen years? He worked, a lot. Late nights, weekends, lots of travel around the country, and always with him was his faithful assistant Margaret. He can't say for sure when it happened, but they found they were quite fond of one another, he and Margaret. And, well, I was the product of that fondness.

"I was born in 1977. Now 1977 was a big year for Honor and Sons. Their first factory had just started rolling product off the line. Major news outlets were following the story as a hundred jobs were created between the factory floor, cleaning crews, trucking crews, and then there were the downstream effects creating jobs in grocery stores and whatnot. It was a big deal. More importantly, Michael was looking to expand beyond regional sales. His factory was overbuilt in hopes that he could up the output rapidly as he courted more national outlets for his cookies. And despite the 1960s and their free love attitude, 1977 was no place for a man with a mistress or a bastard son. And his travel and work schedule never slowed. It was not a schedule any pregnant woman would want to keep, especially with the travel requirements. And so Mom was replaced. She was left jobless and pregnant.

"Which, I'm only guessing here, is why she told me my father was dead and why she never married. I think she didn't want to depend on anyone ever again. I think he broke her heart, and she didn't ever want that to happen again. So in an effort to keep my mom out of the press and out of his life, he offered her 250,000 dollars and all parental rights. To my mother's credit, she didn't use that money but left it all for me and even grew it into a nice sum, as we discussed. I guess she didn't want me to be dependent on anybody either.

"And just like that, she was gone from Michael's life. Seven years later, he's a father again and again three years after that. Turns out, he started to feel remorse for giving up his firstborn, which annoyed his wife to no end, or so he told me, as she had only stayed with him out of a sense of wifely duty when she learned of the whole affair. It was the 1970s. Anyway, he looked for me a little, but Mom changed her name and moved, and he couldn't find us. Jump forward to 2016. He's doing family research for an autobiography he's writing, and he's looking into the Honor family heritage. So he took a Heritage DNA test but didn't make his results or profile public. He did set it to alert him to any new possible familial matches. As he said to me, maybe he'd find a distant cousin who had a tale to tell about the family that would be a worthy anecdote in his book. Imagine his surprise when a son appeared in his alerts. There I was, after all those years, his missing son. He could see that my mother changed her name and moved away from the city and back to her hometown, the name of which she never shared with Michael.

"After that, I didn't have a lot to say, at first, anyway. We ordered lunch. We sat quietly while I took this all in. To his credit, he stayed quiet too and let me process it all. I'm guessing since it was a few weeks after he found out he'd already had time to go through all or at least some of his emotional processing and knew I'd need some time to wrap my head around things. We ate, mostly in silence, with a little small talk about the quality of the food, the quality of the wine, that sort of thing. Afterward, we took coffee. He finally asked if I was okay since I'd hardly said a word since his story.

"And I was okay. I was fine. It was all fine except it wasn't. I wanted to know why he thought this was okay. He bought his way out of my life, and now with his fancy lunch, did he think he could buy his way back into my life? I told him how perfectly happy I had been until about an hour ago when he dropped this bomb on me. Having lost your father to tragedy was sad, but I had accepted it. Now I learned that I lost him because he was an asshole? Well…that's something else. And why now? Why? Would I make a good anecdote for his book? Was I going to be a thrilling chapter at the end? He sat quietly and took it all. I admit, I let the old man have it for a while. Maybe this is why he'd cleared the restaurant. I learned later that he owns the place or did when he was alive.

"When I finally stopped to breathe, he told me he anticipated a lot of what I'd said. He'd thought about it too. He told me he just wanted to know his son, to look him in the eyes and apologize for how he left him, and to ask, if not forgiveness, then acceptance. And with time, he wanted to be part of my life. It could be a quiet part. No mentions in books or papers. I could be a secret from all but those few people who knew. On that note, he cleared the restaurant and had only a few trusted staff on hand. Nobody knew who I was, he swore to it. And he'd done business this way before for VIPs, so it wasn't unusual for him to take a private meeting like this.

"Well, I finished my coffee, thanked him for the meal, and got up to leave, determined never to see the man again. As I was leaving, he handed me a card. It was his personal cell number. He understood if I never called, but if I was interested in meeting again or just talking, I could call. He made a joke and said, 'You might just want to update your doctor with any hereditary illnesses from your father's side. You can call for that too.' I chuckled at this, and he put his hand on my arm. He squeezed tight for just a second, looked in my eyes, and said he was truly sorry. Then he rose, turned, and disappeared through the back door.

"I held onto that card for a few weeks before I called. We met, this time, much more low-key. A park bench with a good view, somewhere just to talk. Over those weeks before I called, my anger had abated. I thought how silly it was to be so angry. That was all the sadness and anger of a young boy without a father coming out. I came to realize I'm a grown man. I'm fine without a father, but what would it hurt to get to know this man? As a child, I'd often dream about my father. I'd ask questions about him, but Mom never said very much. As I got older, I stopped asking. I assumed it was too painful for her to talk about him. When I was much older, I suspected she didn't know him that well. Young lovers, perhaps? And I suppose I was not too far off on that suspicion. And that is why I decided to meet and talk with Michael. I could learn who my father was, answer some lingering question like his favorite baseball player or favorite meal. And for him, I'd be putting his heart at ease knowing I wasn't mad at him. So we met and talked. And the first few times we met, it was just what I wanted—casual conversation, laughs, jokes, stories about Mom, stories about him, stories about me, and stories about my grandfather and uncle. But after a few months and a few meetings, he asked if I'd care to have dinner. There was a tone about the invitation that seemed formal, more serious somehow. I accepted as I was genuinely enjoying my time with Michael.

"I asked where and when we were having dinner. He said he would send a car by my office that day. When I left work, a driver met me and took me to a waiting limo. He opened the door, and there was Michael, waiting for me. Once inside, he told the driver to take a tour of the city. Then he closed the window separating us from the driver and turned off the intercom. He made me turn off my cell phone. I was understandably nervous at this point.

"Michael said to me, 'I'm sorry to spring this on you. It's not like I have a choice though. Stephen, your brother, Joseph, is, well, not the man I'd hoped he'd be. I'll be blunt. He's not CEO material. He's barely middle management material, but that I could work with. It's his drinking, gambling, and womanizing I cannot abide or, more accurately, the board of directors cannot abide. Over the years, I've sold stakes in my company though it is not publicly traded. I own 47 percent of the company. It's not a majority to be sure, but to really outvote me, all the other board members would need to unanimously vote against me, which is very unlikely. But I won't live forever. When I pass on or can no longer perform as CEO, control will pass to my son. And his lack of business acumen combined with his moral failings…the board will vote him out, and they'll take the company public. They'll take control, and that will be the end of my family legacy, our family legacy. My grandfather came to America with a dream. My father grew that dream. I took it further than either of them could have imagined. And now, now I'm set to lose my dream of the Honor family continuing my legacy because my son is bereft of the character necessary to be my successor.'

"I asked Michael why he was telling me all of this. I genuinely did not see what was coming next when he said, 'Because, Stephen, you are a good man. You have an understanding of business. You give back to the community. You're faithfully married. It's not the 1970s anymore. You're rightfully my firstborn son, and I want you to take your place as my successor at Gabriel Industries. I want you to claim your share of the family fortune.'

"I was floored. I politely asked to be let out, and I walked around for hours before heading home. You'd think being offered a fortune would make me ecstatic, but I wasn't. I was pissed off. It felt like he punched me right in the guts. He gave me away, paid to erase me from his family, from his memory, from his life. I was like a stain on a dinner jacket, and he took me to the cleaners, and I was just gone. I actually believed him when he said he felt bad and tried to find me. You know what? I think that was all bullshit. I think he got lucky when I popped up on that Heritage profile. I think our meetings where he just wanted to get to know me was a test. He was looking to see if I was the solution to his problems. His son can't do the job, so he'll use the son he threw away. I was nothing to him once. I was still nothing now, but I had his blood, and that's what he wanted—a bloodline successor. He knows Holly and I can't have children, so I'd have to pass the company to Joseph's kids or Sarah's, if she ever has any. I vowed never to speak to him again. I had plenty of money. I had a great life. That position would be nothing but stress. What's more I found out twice in relatively short order, from my father himself no less, that he has never and will never love me or care about me for being, well, me. He only cares about how I benefit him. I honestly preferred it when I thought my father was dead.

"But I talked it over with Holly. I told her everything I just told you. And she agreed that he was selfish and terrible and that he didn't really care about me. He only cared about his company. Holly did point out that this shouldn't prevent us from benefiting from his misfortune. 'So your brother is a bum. I'd say that is as much nurture as it is nature. Your mom was wonderful, and she raised you to be wonderful too. Who raised your brother? Who taught him to be horrible? So your father did a bad job raising your brother. So he doesn't care about you. Take his money, take his title, and do some good for the world.' With all that money and that position? I could help lots of people. So with Holly's blessing, I called Michael and accepted his offer. We started construction on my dream home, and Michael told me to lay low while he figured out how to make this all work. He didn't say it, but I guessed he wanted to have this deal airtight before going public. No opportunity for a challenge from my brother or the board.

"And then nothing happened. I never heard from him again. I tried calling his cell, then his office. I found out a few weeks after we last talked that he became quite ill. His mind slipped, and he was shut up in his house under constant care and supervision. I found out, like everyone else, that he died by reading the news. And that was that."

Nick sat for a while after Stephen finished his story, taking it all in. "Did your half-siblings know about any of this?"

"I honestly don't know. I never met them, but I don't think Michael told them. I think he told as few people as possible to keep it quiet until he was ready. Then he got sick and died."

"What about Sarah? Why not give her the company?" Nick asked.

"Michael said she's a musician or an actress, something like that, or at least she pretends to be one. He said she has less business in the boardroom than she does on the stage, and he didn't think she belonged on stage either."

"Do you think this is all related?" Holly asked. "Michael kept it quiet," she continued. "After his death, we got nothing. What would be the motivation other than to ruin Stephen? Maybe some grinch just wanted to steal Christmas?"

"It could be unrelated, but Faith Garza is currently being represented in criminal court by a lawyer named Albert Zane. He's working pro bono. He takes on criminal cases from time to time, but that's not his full-time job." Nick paused and could see that Stephen understood.

"Who is Albert Zane?" Holly asked.

Stephen answered, "He's currently the lead corporate and private counsel for Gabriel Industries and the Honor family."

Chapter 14

Snow fell thickly in the waning light of day. It was a wet and heavy snow that clung to the fir trees of the forest surrounding the village, the weight of the snow sagging the evergreen boughs. Darkness came fast and early this evening. The village, usually teeming with activity, was still and silent as the villagers took to their huts early for this was no ordinary night. This night was to be the longest and darkest of the year. Tonight, the villagers huddled in their homes, hoping that the long night would end and that the wheel of time would complete its turn and start again back toward the sun, the warmth of spring, and the abundance of summer.

It was on the longest night of the year that the shaman would take to his hut and begin his trance, taking a journey to see the long hard winter ahead and the spring that was to follow. Tea was drunk, a special blend of herbs that would open him to the spirit world. The shaman chanted and sang, swaying back and forth in the firelight, breathing the smoke of the fire, and feeling the physical world around him disappear. His soul, having departed his body, floated up and out the smoke hole of his hut, and, like the smoke of the fire, drifted in the wind and disappeared into the night.

Deep in the forest, something stirred, something ancient and primal. A hairy beast? Or was it a man? It lumbered through the trees, stepping through the deepening snow, clumps of it clinging to its fur (or was it fur clothing), its back hunched as it walked deliberately through the trees. It sniffed at the distant smell of woodsmoke mixed with the strong scent of pine carried on the winter wind.

The shaman found himself standing in knee-deep snow. Though lightly dressed, he did not feel cold. Rather he felt warm and relaxed, the wet snow making a crunching sound as he stepped, walking without purpose, exploring the forest in which he found himself, slowly became aware of the sound of a second set of muted footfalls in the snow. Ahead in the forest, he saw a shadow passing through the trees. Was it a bear? Or a man? He couldn't be sure. A strong scent of pine filled his nostrils, and he followed, the smell pulling him toward the figure in the snow. The shaman walked, unafraid, having made this journey before. His consciousness caught up with him, and he recognized the figure which he sought, the one that would bring the wheel back around and set the sun on its course back, the one that would end the winter and bring forth the spring.

Finally awake, it became aware that it was a he. He was awake and alive. He was the forest and the winter. He was there for a purpose. He stopped to smell the fresh strong scent of pine and to feel the snow fall on his face. He felt the forest breathe and with him. He was alive in the cold winds of winter. He became aware that he was not alone. Opening his eyes, he saw an old man prostrate on the ground before him. The man rose and looked into his eyes. The man smiled, and he smiled back. The sound of hooves beating through the snow came suddenly, and the wood around them burst into life as reindeer flew past, their ruddy scent filling the air. The wind began to whip through the trees, a sudden gale breaking the stillness. The world had become alive, and magic crackled and sparked as the old man was carried off with the herd, disappearing like smoke in the wind. The sound of bells was jingling, following the herd. He felt the whole world now, not just the forest. He felt it tearing at him, pulling him apart. He could feel himself dying, a sacrifice to bring back the dawn. His heart beat faster and faster, a heat rising within, the wet snow steaming off him. His breaths came in heavy deep draughts, his nostrils flared.

Nick woke with a start, breathless, heart racing. His bedclothes were damp with sweat. It was another fitful night for Nick. This time of year was always hard on his sleep schedule. As the days grew shorter and the weather turned colder, Nick's dreams became increasingly vivid and intense. Underneath it all and despite his best efforts to leave the past behind, Nick was still very much a creature born of winter. No matter how much he tried, he could not deny his true self, especially not as his time approached. He was as much a part of the season as it was of him. His magic was the same that animated the winter and could not be denied as it approached.

He took a hot shower and dressed. Then he remembered what day it was. "Thanksgiving Day," he muttered, settling into an armchair with a cup of hot coffee. He turned on his television. It was an old television, dusty from disuse. The large heavy wooden console TV took up a significant amount of space, its heavy, antiquated cathode-ray tube screen humming as it came to life. A modern flat antenna replaced his old rabbit ears, Nick still having never gone in for cable television. Nick knew he'd eventually have to spring for a more modern flat-screen TV, but with the rare amount of time he spent in front of it, Nick felt he could put off that particular chore for a while longer.

He flipped through the few channels he got, finally settling on the Macy's Parade. Then remembering the day, he topped his coffee off with a shot of whiskey and let his mind wander. Someone had to have figured out Michael Jr.'s plan. There was no way he could pull off what he was planning, giving his entire empire to someone other than Joseph, without help. If he trusted the wrong person and his secret got out, Dash would be a threat to Joseph, which would give him motive. But Michael Jr. died before he moved forward with his plans. There was no mention of Dash in Michael Jr.'s will. As far as Nick could tell, there was no paper trail connecting Michael Jr. and Dash. Even if Joseph did catch wind of his father's plans, it seemed unlikely that he would have gone through with such an elaborate and inherently risky plan to ruin Dash.

Nick wondered, *If not Joseph, then who would benefit from Dash being out of the picture?* Could Holly have been mad enough about Stephen spending their money before securing his father's fortune? No, she was ruined too. Stephen's ruined reputation and possible incarceration left Holly penniless and friendless. It was possible that Stephen had made other enemies, but for the time being, Nick had no other leads. As he mentally returned, he realized the parade was coming to an end. Santa Claus was coming down the road. Nick scowled and turned off the TV.

He went to the computer and started a search on Stephen Dash. The day prior, Nick asked about any possible other enemies. Anyone he had wronged or slighted? Were there any jilted lovers? Did he have any affairs? Anything? But Stephen and Holly only admitted to a happy life and couldn't think of a single person who'd want to do them harm.

"I mean, given what you told me, I'd be suspicious of my half brother, but I'm not sure he even knows about me." Stephen and Holly were adamant that they could think of no one who would want to see Stephen harmed.

Nick searched public records, social media, news articles, class reunions, college alumni newsletters, and anything else with Stephen Dash's name on it. He came up empty. Up until his arrest, Stephen Dash had been a moderately well-off man with a stable job who volunteered for charity, liked to bike, enjoyed time with his wife, and was generally well respected. Nick couldn't find any offense in his criminal record, minor or otherwise. He didn't even have a speeding ticket. The most objectionable thing he could find was Stephen's taste in music and golf attire. Nick decided that was all a matter of personal preference and, more importantly, not likely a motive in his case.

It was late enough in the day now. Nick hit the local diner for Thanksgiving turkey, mashed potatoes, green beans, and pumpkin pie. He took coffee to-go. It was cold out though not as cold as in his dreams. He found a park bench and sat, watching as the bars start to fill up. After a day of excessive food and family, many were driven to excessive drink as well. Nick placed a call to an old friend. "Are you free for a drink?" Nick asked.

"I will be. I'm off duty at seven."

"Paddy's at eight?" Nick asked.

"Paddy's at eight sounds good."

A little after eight, Nick was joined at the bar by a large Black man of indeterminate age. He, like Nick, had the look of an older man and world weary, but his eyes were bright and youthful. He had close-cropped hair that was starting to gray. He was clean-shaven. It was hard to tell, but under his suit, he was well muscled. It was even harder to tell that he was carrying a .45 under his left arm.

"Pete! Can I get you a drink?" Nick asked, greeting his friend merrily.

"Just club soda tonight. I'm on call. Is this business or purely a social call?" Pete asked.

"Can't it be both, Captain?" Nick grinned.

Captain Peter Moore was a second-generation police officer. Like his father before him, Pete joined the force right out of college. Unlike his father, Peter had the luck of living in a slightly more enlightened age. Though hardly perfect, he was spared walking the beat in the "African" neighborhoods his whole career. Patrolman Moore was able to move to detective Moore, then to detective sergeant. It took a while, but he made lieutenant and was recently promoted to captain. His friendship with Nick was long running and almost exclusively professional though Nick had few interactions that weren't work related, and to his credit, Pete knew this.

Pete, Nick had found, was a savvy investigator, willing to think outside the box and, importantly, willing to work with those, like Nick, who were outside the force. Though many disliked private investigators, Pete understood the value of a good source of information regardless of who they were. If Nick helped solve crimes, who cared how he did it as long as it was legal.

"Isn't it always, Nick?" Pete smiled.

"I've got a case and could use some help," Nick said.

Pete silenced him with a finger to his lips. He nodded toward a booth just opening up. Once seated, Pete motioned for Nick to proceed.

"I'm working for Stephen Dash. Are you familiar with the case?"

"I am but it's being handled by the financial crime guys, and since the money went overseas, it's being handed to the FBI. I'd heard you were involved with the shooting of the accountant. What was his name?" Pete took a sip of his soda. "I can't help you there either. I'm a homicide detective, but that is a case for the states. If they think it's tied to the *Dash* case, I'm sure the bureau will pick it up too. So I'm not sure I can be much help."

"I heard the gun used to take out Morgan Wood, that's the accountant, had disappeared from the police evidence lockup," Nick replied.

Pete silenced Nick with a stern look and a finger to his lips. He leaned in close from across the table. "I don't know where you heard about that, but it's an internal affairs investigation. I can't go near that without risking my career, so don't even think about asking me about it."

"Relax. I'm working a different angle. Sort of. I'm connecting some dots, and I came up with six names I need information on. They may have nothing to do with anything, but I was hoping you could give me some background on them?" Nick slid a piece of paper across to Pete.

Pete took a look at the list. "I told you, Nick, I'm not crossing an IA investigation." Pete looked at the list a bit longer. "Are these all cops?" he asked.

"Yeah, they are. Which one is under investigation?"

"Number two. How'd you come up with this list?" Pete asked.

"They've all had some professional trouble, and they've all been represented by the same lawyer," Nick replied.

"And you think this lawyer has something to do with Stephen Dash and Morgan Wood?" Pete raised an eyebrow.

"Right now, he's a common thread. He may or may not be connected, but many of his other clients are. Given what I know of the weapon used in the *Wood* case—"

Pete picked up. "It's prudent to check all cops tied to the lawyer. Got it. All I can say for now is I know that all evidence techs are under investigation as the full evidence inventory is audited. Your number two works the evidence lockup. I don't know much else about her or any of the others, but I'll let you know what I find out. You do remember that my gifts are not given freely, don't you?" He winked at Nick, who rolled his eyes.

"Stephen Dash did not take that money or at least I don't believe he did." Nick then gave an abridged account of the story he heard from Dash.

Pete let out a little whistle at the end. "That's one hell of a story. And I can see his point. Without evidence, it's just a story. Nothing else. No investigator would take it seriously." Pete paused. "Well, no one but you."

Nick smiled.

"I always thought that 'sees you when you're sleeping, knows when you're awake' part was creepy as fuck. You sure you're not a Peeping Tom, are you, Nick?"

Nick's smile faded to a scowl as Pete smiled a big toothy grin. "Your phone is ringing, Pete," Nick said.

Pete reached into his pocket and pulled out his phone. "Captain Moore… Yes, I'll be right over." He hung up the phone. "Say, Nick, I've got to…," he trailed off as he realized Nick was already gone. "I hate it when he does that."

Chapter 15

The next three days Nick spent out of sight. The busiest shopping day of the year and the following weekend were days filled with images of a fat man in a bright-red suit with a great white beard hawking anything and everything under the sun. People dressed in Santa hats and ugly sweaters flocked to malls and big-box stores looking for the best deals. Christmas carols were inescapable. The torment was too much for Nick to bear.

Monday found Nick in better spirits and back on the case. He took his morning papers and coffee in a café located in the lobby of the Pressman Building. The Pressman was an impressive building situated right in the heart of downtown. Built in the city's boom years, it had marbled floors and walls as well as the ornate elevators expected of a building from its era. Its forty floors housed many businesses, including the law offices of Thomas and Yves. And unlike the 12 Tower Way, security was very tight. Fortunately for Nick, a public café took up a portion of the first floor.

Nick settled in and read the paper. He sipped his hot coffee, and he watched people. His weekend in seclusion was not unproductive as he was able to do his homework, finding, among other things, corporate photographs of the staff of Thomas and Yves on their website.

Nick thought it was wonderful how everyone these days would just tell you where they work, where they went to school, and what they like to eat. *It used to be so much harder to find people*, Nick thought. Nick spent the rest of the morning watching for employees of Thomas and Yves as they come and go. He'd love to talk with either senior partner, but he had a suspicion they won't use the front door or spend their free time taking coffee from paper cups in the lobby. But he was betting on the three newest members of the team passing through the public space he now occupied. He was also hoping one of them would be more loose-lipped than a seasoned attorney might.

Around 10:30 a.m., Lila Gestirn came to the café for coffee. She ordered a seasonal latte, extra peppermint and white chocolate shavings, and took a seat at the high top table near the window. Lila Gestirn was thirty years old, a graduate of George Washington Law School. At twenty-eight, she graduated near the top of her class and went on to clerk for an appellate judge for a year before being hired by Thomas and Yves.

Nick tucked his papers under his arm and folded his coat over his forearm. He took his drink and approached Lila. She jumped, startled from her midmorning reverie, when Nick asked if the other seat was taken.

Lila replied, "It's not, but you could sit somewhere else. There's another empty table behind you."

Nick smiled. "I could but I was hoping to speak with you, Ms. Gestirn."

"If you're looking for legal advice, you need to go through our usual referral process."

Nick replied, "Oh, no. I'm not looking for an advice. I'm looking for some answers. I'm a private investigator, Nick Saint." He extended his hand, and they shook.

"Take a seat, but I can't discuss any of my clients, so you're probably going to be disappointed."

Nick sat. "I was hoping to find out about a former client, Michael Honor Jr."

"That fiasco? I was just starting when the account was transferred. I know it was a huge deal though. Not only had Thomas and Yves represented the Honor family's interests since the '70s, but they were also trying to keep it in the family. They couldn't stop the account from leaving though, and I was just lucky to have kept my job."

"Why were you lucky to have kept your job?" Nick asked.

"Well, the loss of Gabriel Industries and the Honor family was a huge financial hit to the firm. They had to scale back. They had to. I thought being so green, I'd be cut for sure, but they bought out a bunch of the senior execs. Those making the most, I guess. They cut them sweet severance packages, and away they went to retirement or wherever old lawyers go. If we were going to court new business, then we didn't need all those senior attorneys. We needed a few strategists at the top and a bunch of cheap labor to do all the grunt work, paper pushers. And that was me. I may have been just cheap labor, but still, I felt lucky." Lila sipped her drink. "What's this all about anyway?" she asked.

"I'm looking into a case with a connection to the Honor family and to their new law firm. I thought a little history might be informative. Just one more question, if you don't mind?"

"Shoot," Lila said.

"You said the firm was trying to keep the company in the Honor family. Who were they trying to put in charge? Since Joseph took the company to Rich and Wellhoff, there must've been someone else they were trying to install as CEO and chairman of the board."

Lila stared at Nick for a moment. "That's all wrong, Nick. Joseph was working with us to keep his position. His dad was ill, but there wasn't a provision for anyone to vote in his stead should he be absent due to illness or any other reason. He was 47 percent of the vote. Joseph had assumed operational control when his dad fell ill by nature of his name. No one questioned it, I guess. But with Michael Jr. ill, the board moved to Rich and Wellhoff, and no one could stop them. We were working to stop any transactions until a replacement could be found to represent the Honor family's interests with the board, but the board moved faster than we did. Since the Honor family didn't have any legally binding paperwork allowing for a proxy to vote for Michael, he legally abstained from voting when he fell ill, and the board was able to do whatever it liked. Lucky for the family, the old man died, and his will passed control of the company and his board seat to his son."

Nick thanked Lila for her time and gave her his card. He asked that she pass it on to her senior partners. He told her he might be able to get the Honor family account back for them and that she could be the hero of the firm if she passed the message on. She had said she would think about it and then headed back to the elevators, and Nick returned to his papers.

Just before noon, Nick packed up to leave the café in search of lunch and to plot his next move when his phone rang. "Hello? Mr. Saint? I'm Richard, Mr. Thomas's assistant. He wishes to invite you to lunch with Ms. Yves and himself. Would today at one work for you?"

Nick thought, *That was quick*. Then he answered, "Sure. I'm close by. Where shall I meet them?"

"We have an executive dining area on our floors. I'll be down to collect you at ten minutes til," Richard replied.

At one, Nick was seated in a comfortable dining area, his hat and jacket taken at the door. Mr. Thomas and Ms. Yves entered and were seated across the table from him. Introductions were made by Richard who then excused himself and exited the room. Once appetizers were served, all the staff left the dining room.

"Okay, Mr. Saint," Mr. Thomas began, "you have our attention. Tell us how you can get Gabriel Industries and the Honor family back."

"I have some questions first. You answer mine and I can more fully answer yours." Nick waited while Mr. Thomas and Ms. Yves conferred.

"Okay, we accept under the condition you tell us everything you know."

Now it was Nick's turn to think. "If I can hold back a few names, for now, to protect my client, then we have a deal."

The two lawyers exchanged a brief glance before saying together, "You have a deal."

"You represented the Honor family and Gabriel Industries since the '70s, correct?"

"Correct. Michael had the vision and drive to take the family business and turn it into an empire. We had the ability to make that dream real and to protect it. If he was the ship's captain, we were the navigators and the marines. We plotted the course and repelled all invaders," Mr. Thomas said.

Nick noted the globe and anchor tiepin. *Once a marine, always a marine*, Nick thought.

"So losing to Rich and Wellhoff, it was more than a financial loss, I take it?"

"Much more. That was as much our company as anybody. We helped take the bakery national, then set about all the other investments that came to make up Gabriel Industries," Ms. Yves said.

"So you were integral to the company. You were not only close advisors to the CEO, both personally and professionally, but you also put together most, if not all, the legal framework upon which the company was built. Am I correct?"

"You are correct," Ms. Yves said.

"Why then would the board wish to cut you out? Who knows the company better than you two and your office?"

Yves and Thomas exchanged a look and a few whispers. Then Ms. Yves said, "Because we are as loyal to the Honor family as we are to the company. We watched the company grow alongside Joseph and Sarah. No matter what, we want the Honor children to retain control of their legacy. The board, on the other hand, are venture capitalists, wealthy investors, former owners of companies absorbed by Gabriel Industries when they vertically integrated."

Nick raised an eyebrow. "Vertically integrated?" Nick asked.

"Michael took control of all aspects of his business from wheat and sugar crops to the distribution truck lines. When he would buy out, say, a wheat mill or a trucking company, sometimes a board seat was part of the sale. The board wanted to take the company public. An IPO would net them huge amounts of money. Michael would not even consider going public."

Nick sat for a moment, thinking. "Did Joseph want that?" he asked.

"Not that we know of, but his father, though ill, was still alive at the time. Joseph had no voting rights, so we don't really know his intentions. Still, we were working to get Michael's board seat and voting rights transferred to Joseph. With his dad alive, I don't think he'd have voted to go public. After his death? Who knows."

"And if he didn't want to, couldn't he block the vote?" Nick asked.

"For a while, but he had certain moral failings, and he's honestly terrible at running a business. His dad moved him around to different divisions with varying responsibilities, trying to give him a chance to find his way, but Joseph inevitably tanked whatever he was working on. Mostly, he doesn't have the business acumen necessary to run such a large company. It does help that he spends too much time gambling, drinking, and chasing women. The board would eventually vote him out. It would take time and effort to get a majority to vote against Joseph, but they eventually would. Joseph would screw up badly enough that even the board members loyal to the family would be forced to vote him out to save the company. So with Michael sick, the board members who wanted to go public had enough votes to do it without getting every single board member behind it. They tried moving fast to get things in motion to take the company public. Then Michael died, and Joseph was able to slow things down."

"Why did Joseph take the family accounts to Rich and Wellhoff then, if you were trying to help him?" Nick asked.

"His family affairs are so tangled up with the company, we couldn't advise him well once we lost access to whatever was going on with the company. If he went with Rich and Wellhoff and they worked to undermine his personal interests, he could sue them and claim the work they did for the board to oust him was a conflict of interest and get a judge to slow or overturn any board decisions. At the very least, he could tie everyone up in legal proceedings for a while, so we advised him to go."

"You advised him to go?" Nick asked, surprised.

"For his own best interests, we did. I told you, Mr. Saint, we're loyal to the company and the family. We couldn't protect him or advise him properly anymore. But put him personally and professionally in the Rich and Wellhoff portfolio and at least he would have a chance."

"Why hadn't Michael made provisions for someone to take his seat if he was ever incapacitated?"

"We're not sure. We advised him to do so, but I know he didn't think Joseph was ready. He could've used a surrogate that wasn't Joseph, but he never did."

"Did Michael ever mention leaving the company to anyone other than Joseph? Maybe Sarah?"

The two exchanged whispers, heated at times, while Nick sat and waited. The appetizers were first-rate, he noted. After a lengthy deliberation, Ms. Yves spoke, "We know that Michael never considered his daughter for a leadership role. She is a wonderful woman, but her interests lay in the theater and on the stage, not in the boardroom. Michael loved his daughter but knew her strengths and desires. She wouldn't have been a good fit for the role, and she wouldn't have wanted it anyway. As for someone else..." Ms. Yves paused.

Mr. Thomas picked up where she left off, "Michael had us change a portion of his will, leaving his board seat and control of the company to a third party as well as adding this party to the family trust, which would've reduced the holdings of the other beneficiaries significantly."

"Who was this thirty party?" Nick asked.

"We don't know. Michael asked that we keep the changes in strict confidence. We personally handled the work. When completed, he had several copies made, presumably to be reviewed and distributed to his family, but the name of the individual was left blank. We're not sure if he found someone or was hopeful to find someone. We assumed he would come back with a completed document for us to execute in the event of his death. He never did. Michael became ill, and Joseph began handling his father's business affairs and the rest we already told you."

Nick sat thinking for a few minutes. "Was Michael in poor health? He wasn't particularly old when this all happened."

"Not that we know of, but we know he had some heart condition. It kept him out of the army, so it could be he wasn't destined for a long life." There was a buzz at the door.

"That's lunch," Mr. Thomas said.

The conversation paused as waitstaff cleared the appetizers and served lunch. Nick and his hosts ate, mostly in silence, allowing the waitstaff to remain. After the meal, coffee was served, and the waitstaff once again left.

"Okay, Mr. Saint, it's your turn. Tell us what you know."

"As I said, to protect my client, for now, I am keeping his name, but I believe he is the unnamed third party Michael had in mind. He has told me an incredible story that would suggest as much. However, aside from his word, there is no other evidence to support the story or, should I say, no evidence that I am in possession of. I took his case because he is accused of a crime that, despite damning evidence against him, I believe him to be innocent of. I had already found connections to Albert Zane, interim CEO at Rich and Wellhoff, prior to hearing my client's account of his meetings with Michael Honor. Once I knew about my client's connection to Michael Honor and his potential as successor to Michael Honor, I found a damn good motive to frame my client." Nick paused to drink his coffee.

"That all sounds wonderful, but, as you have said, there's no evidence to corroborate his story. So how does this help us?" Mr. Thomas asked.

"I said there's no evidence that I'm in possession of…but if no evidence existed anywhere, no one would've known about my client nor had reason to frame him for a crime to get him out of the way. My guess is the evidence exists. I just need to find it."

"And if these supposed perpetrators that framed your client had said evidence, wouldn't they just destroy it and leave your client alone?" Ms. Yves asked.

"I'm sure they would or did destroy the evidence they found, but—this is just my working theory—they either couldn't be sure they destroyed every copy of the evidence or they know they didn't."

Mr. Thomas and Ms. Yves were quiet for a few minutes. They again conferred in whispered voices.

It must be a courtroom skill, Nick thought as he watched the hushed debate.

"What do you need from us then?"

Nick smiled. "Oh, ho, ho, ho." Nick laughed. "You two are quick."

Chapter 16

Nick had hoped that his conversation with Thomas and Yves would have narrowed his suspect list, but it only broadened it. Any member of the board wishing to publicly offer the company and being blocked would certainly have a financial incentive to keep Stephen Dash out of the picture. But how would any of them have heard of Dash? And his half brother and sister each had personal and financial motivation to keep Dash from taking over.

Nick rolled the possibilities over in his mind, unable to sleep well, partly due to the case but mostly due to his increasingly vivid dreams of vast white plains, cold evergreen forest, and the *jing-jing-a-ling* of sleigh bells. Bleary-eyed and stiff, Nick rose from bed early on Tuesday. He traded his suit for matching navy blue trousers and a long-sleeve button-down shirt, typical of the uniform worn by janitors and maintenance workers. He grabbed a tool kit that held the usual array of hammers, saws, drills and bits, and screwdrivers. It also contained, in a secret compartment, the not-so-usual array of tools like picks and rakes to open doors that someone wished would remain closed.

Nick took the bus uptown from his office, where, among the shops and fine dining, one could also find high-rent apartments and condominiums or, in the case of Joseph Honor, a penthouse suite. Joseph, though married and having never admitted it publicly, was well-known to have been separated from his wife, who returned to live with her family in Connecticut, taking their children along with her. Joseph was also well-known for his gambling, drinking, and womanizing despite having a small, loyal, and discrete domestic staff.

Nick entered the ten-floor office building, the tenth floor of which contained Joseph's apartment and only his apartment, through a service entrance that, despite the signs not to prop open, was currently propped open with a brick. Nick slipped into the private garage and found the elevator. Nick looked about the garage and found a darkened corner where he could wait unseen. After an hour of waiting, a black Mercedes SUV pulled into the garage. Two men, the driver and a front-seat passenger, exited the vehicle. The driver left the engine running. They briefly searched the surrounding area, overlooking Nick as though he were part of the darkness in the corner. The men then positioned themselves, one by the elevator and the other by the back passenger door of the SUV.

Five minutes later, the elevator door opened for Joseph Honor, who was escorted to the Mercedes by the waiting man. The other opened the door, and Joseph climbed quickly into the back seat. He shut the door and returned to the driver's seat while the other returned to the front passenger seat. The vehicle then exited the garage.

Nick waited until the Mercedes was out of sight, then called the elevator. He entered the elevator and could see the button for the tenth floor where Joseph lived, but to access the tenth floor, it required a key. Unable to access the tenth floor directly, Nick took the elevator to the ninth. He paused after exiting the elevator. Looking around the ninth floor, Nick found the emergency stairwell with rooftop access.

The wind, cold and biting in the early morning light, exhilarated Nick as he turned to face it directly, letting it blow hard and directly into his face. He took a deep breath and enjoyed the view as the city came to life below him. Nick returned to the job at hand, looking for the rooftop unit, the combined air-conditioning and heating unit that supplied the penthouse. Nick found the electric panel and powered down the system. He then found the ducting into the penthouse. Nick opened his toolbox and removed a hammer. He banged on the ductwork in a rhythmic pattern, hoping the noise would carry down into the penthouse.

After a few minutes, Nick returned his hammer to his toolbox. On his way to the stairwell, Nick stopped. "Oh, ho, ho." He laughed, taking the lineman's tool from his box to sever the main fiber optic cable supplying the building with Internet, television, and telephone services. He then continued down the stairs to the tenth floor.

From the stairwell, he was able to knock on the door to the penthouse. After a moment, a maid named Carol opened the door, rather confused at having a visitor approach from the emergency stairwell. Nick apologized for the noise and inconvenience but let Carol know that he could not restore heat until he was sure there was no water leaking into the penthouse.

"See, these newer furnaces burn very efficiently. They used to only get about 80 percent efficiency. Now they're up into the high 90s. But water vapor needs to be removed from the system instead of being let out with the exhaust. It wouldn't be much of an issue except for, well, the unit supplying this penthouse is huge, and the water drains off the roof into the rainwater system. I was doing a routine maintenance check and found that the runoff pipe had burst and was just leaking underneath the rubber matting on the roof. It was just pooling underneath the weather proofing. I can't fix the pipe. I'm just with building maintenance. I've got a call into the heating guys to fix the pipe and to the roofers. It looks like this has been going on for a while. See that same pipe is busy in the summer too, getting rid of the water vapor from the AC condenser.

"Anyway, there were signs of rot on the roof, and I'm afraid it's been leaking into your ceiling. I can't turn the heat back on if it's just going to be draining water into your ceiling and doing even more damage. If I can confirm it's not, I'll be able to get the heat back on right away. If it is leaking into the penthouse, well then, we'll have to wait until the HVAC guys get out here later today to repair the pipe."

Carol was unsure what she should do in this situation. Management would usually call about these things first, and maintenance would usually come through the lobby entrance from the elevator. Still, he was just on the roof, no doubt about that. She could tell by his wind-reddened cheeks and the fact that there had been noises coming from the ductwork, just as he said. Carol, waffling at the door, turned to look for some assistance from the other household staff. The chef and valet agreed to let Nick in. Neither wished to tell Mr. Honor he had water damage. Best to let the man look, and if he found anything, it could be his job to tell Mr. Honor.

Nick was given free rein of the property to examine though he was being closely and carefully watched by a dubious Carol. Nick began by passing through every room with his eyes toward the ceiling. Then he walked through again, sounding the ceiling by tapping with a broom handle, which Carol reluctantly let him borrow.

"Wet plaster sounds different," he had told her. Several times he stopped in the bedroom, the office, and the den to sound more vigorously and listen more carefully. Afterward, Nick told Carol he just need to be safe and tap a small hole in the ceilings of a few rooms and insert a camera. He was likely not to find anything, but he couldn't be certain.

This was too much for Carol who did not want to take responsibility for any damage done to her boss's home. She would be calling the building manager, thank you very much. In her disagreeable state, she walked off, leaving Nick alone while she telephoned the front desk, which was currently out of order, thanks to Nick.

Without the ever-vigilant Carol by his side, Nick quickly set to work. Inside Joseph's private study, he moved quietly, opening drawers, checking waste bins, and looking for anything hidden away. He found a locked cabinet which, thanks to his picks, didn't stay locked for long. Inside, he found the prospectus for the Little Drummer Boy. *Joseph knew about the charity, but what else did he know?* Nick wondered as he used his phone to quickly snap photos of every page. He found similar prospectuses in the folder for a range of other nonprofits. Nick quickly snapped their names in case any are connected. Farther back in the drawer, he found a copy of his father's will and his mother's along with her power of attorney documents. He also found a copy of his father's complete medical record and an independent autopsy report that was completed by the hospital pathologist.

Why would he have these? It wouldn't be unusual to have some medical documentation regarding his father, but a several-hundred-page complete copy? Nick won't have time to look through anything this lengthy, but he was able to copy the autopsy report.

With the sound of Carol coming down the hall, Nick put the room back how he found it and quickly slipped out of the study and back into the bedroom. Carol returned to find Nick with a flexible camera inside the air vent.

"Good news!" Nick announced. "No water leaks, and I was able to tap the hole in the air duct, so no visible damage done. I'll even seal it up as I leave. I hope the building manager was able to address your concerns?"

"No, he wasn't available. Apparently, the Internet and cable is out to the building," Carol replied.

"Well, that's telecoms, all zeros and ones. This is more of a plumbing problem, all Hs and Os." Nick laughed at his own joke, but Carol did not appear amused. "I'll see myself out," Nick said.

Carol had other ideas and escorted Nick out the door. Nick returned to the rooftop and restored power to the rooftop unit. It fired up immediately, the thermostat inside having dropped several degrees during Nick's search of the penthouse. Then Nick took the stairs back to the maintenance area. From there, he exited the building through the same door, still propped open, and headed for the bus. Back home, Nick printed out copies of all the photos he took but had no time to review them. He had a ticket to the theater and didn't want to miss the show.

Chapter 17

Tiny Tim, atop Scrooge's shoulders, "God bless us, everyone." The lights went up on the stage, and the orchestra began to play. The supporting cast began to sing and were joined by the main cast as they took the stage one by one. The audience rose, clapping—a standing ovation for the performance. They cheered and whistled with a crescendo every time another of the main cast would enter the stage to take a bow. Finally, the director entered to join the cast as they all bow to a rousing and prolonged ovation.

Nick was seated in the back of the theater, his ticket a last-minute acquisition from an old friend. He, like the rest of the audience, was on his feet, clapping. Though he thought Fezziwig was a bit flat and Tiny Tim was, for some reason, unlikeable, overall, he thought it was an excellent performance, one Charlie Dickens would've been happy to see.

After the performance, Nick roamed the lobby of the theater. The audience, by and large, went scrambling for the doors, headed for dinner, home, or perhaps to the Christkindlmarket in the old town square to shop for Christmas gifts. The faux German advent market was the centerpiece of the downtown Christmas experience. It was within walking distance of the theater district and a popular destination. A recreation of an alpine village with shops selling ornaments, sweaters, blankets, chocolates, nuts, coffee, tea, spices, and other unique and festive items filled the old town square, now just a small block surrounded by the towering skyscrapers of a modern city. Nearby the city holiday tree and ice rink was surrounded by restaurants. Holiday shoppers, couples on dates, and families fresh from the theater or ballet flocked to this area to smell the chestnuts roasting, taste the hot chocolate, and generally continue making merry.

A number of guests remained outside the masses, trying to push out of the building. This smaller crowd perused the show merchandise: sweatshirts, pins, magnets, tree ornaments, coffee mugs, and copies of Dickens original *Christmas Carol*. Trinkets to remember a wonderful time drew many but so, too, was the knowledge that the performers would often stop by to greet fans and sign autographs. Many of the cast members were local performers, but often Scrooge and Bob Cratchit had more national renown.

Nick turned over some merchandise, inspecting the quality and price. He browsed while watching the crowd. A small buzz rose as Fezziwig and Marley enter. Nick was hoping Sarah Honor—director, producer, and theater owner—would make an appearance as she was often reputed to do, but she did not this evening. After thirty minutes, ushers politely cleared the lobby, and the actors sent their fans off with many well-wishes for the holiday season.

Nick circled to the back of the building, looking for a place he may be able to catch Sarah Honor and ask her a few questions. He recognized a few actors from the show exiting a door in the rear of the building. They crossed the alley to a private parking lot. It was unattended but did have an automatic security gate. Nick found a spot to wait, a small alcove in the alley, the service entry to a currently unoccupied storefront. For an hour, the actors trickled out in twos and threes. After ninety minutes, with just one car left in the lot, a 2017 black BMW sedan, Sarah Honor exited and crossed the alley into the parking lot. Nick stepped from the shadows and headed toward Sarah. He stopped short when he heard two other people walking across the parking lot toward Sarah from the other side of the lot. He could hear a man's voice calling out to Sarah, but Nick could not hear what she said in response. For a few moments, Nick could hear a muffled but tense conversation as he tried to move quietly through the alley into a position to see without being seen.

Coming to the corner of the parking lot and the adjacent building, Nick was able to peer around the corner. Sarah was standing toe to toe with a White man in a dark-blue suit. He stood about a head taller than Sarah, maybe six feet tall. He was broad shouldered and had thick limbs. He was clean-shaven and had salt-and-pepper hair and green eyes. He had a scar on his left cheek. He and Sarah were having a heated argument. The other person was also a man, younger than the first, maybe twenty but no more than twenty-five years old. He was wearing a similar blue suit that hung from his body, his wiry frame not filling out the suit as well as his partner. He had a neatly trimmed beard, close-cropped dark-brown, almost-black hair, and brown eyes. He remained quiet but slowly moved around to Sarah's left side.

Suddenly, the tall man grabbed Sarah's shoulder, and she yelled out, pulling away from her assailant, causing his jacket to open, and Nick saw the outline of a gun on his hip. Nick broke into a sprint. The sound of his heavy footfalls caught the attention of the trio. They stopped and looked at Nick. Then the two men turned to run back across the lot and out into the street.

Nick stopped when he reached Sarah. "Are you okay?" he asked, slightly out of breath.

"I'm...I'm fine. Just shaken and surprised. A good surprise though, not them but you, a Good Samaritan at Christmas, my savior," Sarah rambled on for a moment, nervously looking around.

"I think they're gone. Did you know those guys? It looked like you were having an argument when that guy grabbed you."

"We were arguing, and I don't really know him. An actor I rejected came to give me a critique of tonight's performance. Actors can be such drama queens, but Ben Brantley, he is not. Anyway... thank you, Mr.?"

"Saint, Nick Saint."

"What a festive name, Mr. Saint. How can I ever repay you?" Sarah asked.

"You could answer a few questions for me, Ms. Honor."

Sarah's face tightened. "You're not a reporter, are you? I'm not doing private interviews. My publicist has a press packet. You can call her in the morning."

"No, no, nothing like that. I'm a private investigator."

"Oh, a private I? So your rescue wasn't just divine providence? Just a lucky coincidence?" Sarah said.

"Call it an early Christmas gift," Nick said.

"Okay then, Private I, what do you want to know?"

"Does the name Faith Garza mean anything to you?"

Sarah's brow furrowed as she thought. "I don't recall it. Why?"

"How about Robyn Goode?" Nick asked.

"Still no, sorry. Should I know them?"

"What about the Little Drummer Boy charity?" Nick asked.

"Oh, that? Yes, I'm familiar with that. I'm on the board of the Honor Family Charitable Trust. My mother turned to philanthropy after my father made his fortune and the life of a socialite became boring. At the urging of my father, I took her board seat after she became unwell. He was never really involved with the organization, but since my mom started it, he thought the family should be represented on the board. So I did it, for Mom though. It is her legacy and was her passion. I didn't do it to appease my father. I'm not very involved, if I am being honest, but the Little Drummer Boy was discussed for a grant proposal. Then they had some bad publicity recently, a theft of funds, I think? If I recall, the perpetrator is in jail now."

"Mostly correct," Nick replied. "One of the alleged perpetrators is at home on house arrest awaiting trial. The other is dead."

"That's right. It was the accountant that was killed. Is that correct? I am trying to remember what I heard on the news. What does this have to do with me?" Sarah asked as she unlocked her car with the fob and used the remote start to turn the engine over.

"I represent the other alleged perpetrator, the treasurer. I believe he is innocent, set up by Faith Garza, a.k.a. Robyn Goode, and her boyfriend, Morgan Wood, the deceased accountant."

"And what, pray tell, does this have to do with me?" Sarah opened the door to her car.

"Faith was known to be a bartender nearby. She had a reputation for taking home talented men."

"I thought she had a boyfriend?" Sarah asked.

"She did until he got himself killed. I figure she may be trying to get back with an old flame. Her payday was ruined when Wood died, so she needs to find another cash cow."

"And you think she's with one of my actors?"

"I'm checking around town. If one of your troop was suddenly not acting like themselves or Faith was hanging around, I'd like to believe you'd have known about it," Nick said.

"Well, nothing comes to mind, Nick. And now, I'd like to go home." Sarah slid into the driver's seat and shut her door.

Nick knocked on the window. She rolled it down, and Nick handed her his card. "Call me if you hear anything?" She took his card and pulled away into the night.

Chapter 18

"Rudy! Over here!" Nick called from a booth in the back corner of Sunny's Side Up, a hole-in-the-wall diner that was Nick's favorite breakfast in the city. The food was best described as greasy American—heavy on the meat and cheese, light on the vegetables, with almost comically large portion sizes.

Rudy squeezed past the tightly packed tables and into the open seat at the back table that Nick had kicked out with his foot. "Thanks for meeting me. Did you get the info I asked for?"

"I did, Nick, but honestly, most of this you could've found with a Google search. I'm pretty sure that's how Diane found it," Rudy said.

"Diane?" Nick asked.

"Yeah, she's the new editor for the society and arts pages."

"What happened to Molly? I liked her."

"She moved to New York, took a job with *The Times*. Did you ever meet Molly?" Rudy asked.

"No, I never met her, but she always had good information for me."

"Correction. I always have good information for you, Nick. I vet the stuff before I pass it along."

"Fair enough." Nick paused while two heaping plates were laid out in front of them. Four sunny-side up eggs, three pieces of bacon, two sausage links, two pieces of toast, home fries, and a waffle with an ice cream scoop of butter on top and a full cup of hot syrup on the side. The waitress topped off Nick's coffee and poured a fresh cup for Rudy.

"You know I'm not going to eat that, right?" Rudy said, his stomach turning just thinking about eating even half of it. "My doctor is watching my LDL. You should too, you know. You're not getting any younger." Rudy smiled at Nick, who was eating with vigor.

"If I ever saw a doctor, I'm not sure they'd know what to do with me. And I don't think cholesterol is going to get me," Nick replied between mouthfuls of food.

"Okay, fair enough. You eat. I'll talk. You will tell me why you want this information, won't you?" Nick nodded while chewing. "So the Honor boy, Joseph, is separated from his wife but still legally married. The family has kept it mostly quiet but couldn't hide all of it. They maintain separate residences, but Joseph visits regularly to see his kids. They're five and seven. It is only a rumor, but the word is that Joseph drinks, gambles, and chases women. He apparently got sloppy though and someone caught him, on film, with someone other than his wife. Now it probably wasn't the first or the last time he'll be unfaithful, but this was likely the first time there was public proof which would be an embarrassment to his wife and reason to separate. There was a prenup signed, the contents of which are not public. But if she's staying, I'm guessing it's because she'll lose everything if she doesn't. Business wise, he's a mess. His father bounced him around, but whatever he put him in charge of had trouble likely because he spent more time drinking than working." Rudy took a pause to fix his coffee—one sugar and two creamers.

Nick paused eating to ask, "So why keep him on in the family business? Why not bring in the daughter? Or someone else?"

Rudy sipped his coffee, nodding approvingly at the taste. "Great question. No one knows why except for a few years ago, Sarah famously declared during a *60 Minutes* interview that she wanted no part of the family business. She said, 'Leave the dynasty to Joseph. I'll make my own.' She opened her own theater shortly after. She tried and did okay as an actress, off Broadway productions, nothing big. Her critical reviews were mediocre at best. She was never written off as terrible. She was just not likely to win any awards. She wrote a few plays and funded them in some small theaters. Again, similar reactions. Critics thought the performances were good, but the stories left something to be desired. Her theater though does quite well. She took on directorial duties and stopped writing and acting. She had the money to buy a few decent scripts and has kept the place running."

Nick finished his plate. "That's it?" he asked.

"That's it."

Nick thought for a few minutes. "Did she ever want to be part of the family business?"

"As far as I know, never. She never even had a summer job there or an internship when she went to business school."

"She has a business degree?" Nick asked.

"Yeah, an MBA. Her undergrad was in theater, but she went back for an MBA before opening the theater." Nick was silent for a while. Rudy broke the silence. "Is this still about the *Stephen Dash* case? Or are you working on something new?"

Nick, startled from deep thought, answered, "It is still about Stephen Dash. Look, the Honor family is somehow wrapped up in all of this: Wood's death and Dash being set up. Everything is connected. I just don't know how yet."

Rudy took a turn being silent, lost in thought. Nick asked, "Anything about Michael Honor Jr.?"

"Very little. He disappeared from public sight last year. The family rep said he was ill, and that's about it. We don't hear from him again until his family announces his passing."

Nick rested his elbows on the table, palms together, tapping his index fingers.

"Oh, Diane said there was an unnamed source close to the family that said he had dementia or Alzheimer's, that he was having hallucinations, an inability to remember, outbursts, forgetfulness, and lethargy, but nobody would confirm it. When the paper started asking around, the Honor family lawyer sent a letter asking us to respect the Honor family's privacy and further action would be taken if we pressed the issue. It wasn't a front-page exposé, just a minor filler piece for the society page. We dropped it and never corroborated the story."

Nick dropped a fifty on the table. He stood to put on his coat. "Well, Rudy, I may have front page for you. Just be ready for my call."

*****

Back at his office, Nick was pacing when the intercom buzzed. Nick pushed the button to unlock the door, and he could hear the heavy footfalls of Pete Moore coming down the hall. Pete entered and dropped a file folder on Nick's desk. He turned and went to the shelf where Nick kept a bottle of whiskey and some glasses. He filled one and motioned to Nick.

"None for me, thanks. Still too early," Nick said.

"Not if you work night shift," Pete said. He sat down.

Nick took a seat and started to flip through the several-inch-thick file Pete had left. "Where's the Cliff's notes?"

"Aww, man, Twitter has spoiled you. You used to take your time with these things. You used to like to take in all the details." Pete laughed.

"First of all, Peter, I do not tweet, and I still like the details. But this?" Nick held up the heavy file folder. "This is like *War and Peace*."

"Okay, fine. I'll summarize for you. Of the six guys you gave me—one is dead, old age. One is retired, living in Florida. And one is in a nursing home, early onset Alzheimer's. Now we get to the good stuff. The remaining three were all charged together for assaulting a prisoner. This was a number of years ago, pre-body camera but not pre-smartphone. Someone recorded the incident. The senior officer on scene was Sergeant Victor 'Mack' MacArthur. He arrived to back up Penny Ambrose. The victim was a rather large and rather intoxicated member of The Family, a well-known biker gang. He was causing a disturbance at a TGI Friday's. Apparently, he had a few drinks with the gang before going to see his daughter for a dinner date.

"After a few more drinks, he became belligerent and fought with the waitstaff and some other patrons. Corporal Ambrose arrived first and tried to verbally de-escalate, but he charged her and took her to the ground. They fought, and she was able to subdue him but had yet to put on the cuffs. Enter Sergeant Mack. The now subdued man who had ceased to fight was lying still under Ambrose who had him pinned to the floor. Mack kicked him in the face and ribs repeatedly. Ambrose did not physically try to stop him but yelled for Mack to stop so she could cuff him. The rookie officer, still in his probationary on-the-job training, Sebastian Henwood, was riding along with Mack. He tried several times to stop Mack by trying to place himself between the two, but after being chastised by Mack and Ambrose, he shied away from further attempts. A call from a panicked bystander to 911 got a lieutenant on the scene who took over and relieved Sergeant Mack. Video of the incident hit the news, and an investigation was opened. All three were charged with assaulting a prisoner.

"The lawyer you mentioned, Zane? He took the case. Mack unfortunately lost his job and served twelve months' probation. Ambrose was assigned to the evidence lockup, which is like a glorified security guard. And Henwood? Well, he was cleared of all charges. Given his feeble attempts to stop the violence and his inexperience, he was deemed not at fault or a party to the act. He was transferred to another precinct and, get this, is now a detective in the narcotics unit."

Nick went to the shelf and poured himself a drink. "What happened to Mack?"

"He took a job doing security work and also became a private investigator. Who would hire a disgraced police officer to be a security guard and private investigator, you ask? Great question. Turns out, lots of people. His violent tendencies really endear him to certain clientele."

"Anyone I would know or want to know about?" Nick asked.

"Sorry, that's beyond a summary. Everyone I know of that he worked for is in that file."

"So a gun from a drug bust goes missing from evidence and is used to kill someone who may have been set up by a billionaire client of the lawyer they all share?"

"Yep," Peter said before downing his drink.

"That's a big coincidence, don't you think?" Nick asked.

"I don't think anything, Nick. Not yet. Bring me something concrete, and I'll do more than think. Until then, I'm going to bed. Thanks for the drink."

Chapter 19

Sebastian Henwood, thirty-two years old, was a narcotics detective in the first ward police department. He was promoted two years ago, having shown himself to be a capable investigator and was instrumental in the reduction of drug trafficking and the associated violent and nonviolent crime in the ward. Twice he was commended for bravery in the line of duty. He was known for his work ethic and integrity. He was well-liked by both his fellow officers and the citizens of the community. Detective Henwood was an outstanding member of the police force and a credit to his badge. As a rookie officer, still in training with a sergeant from the third ward, Detective Henwood was involved in an incident in which a detained suspect (who was later charged with resisting arrest, assault of an officer, public intoxication, drug possession, and illegal weapons possession) was struck by the foot of his training sergeant in the face and ribs during an attempt to restrain and cuff the subject. An inquiry and later a trial found Detective Henwood was not at fault or in any way negligent or responsible for any injury sustained by the suspect. Given his status as a rookie officer still in training, he was reinstated to duty and transferred to the first ward. He repeated all prior weeks of his departmental orientation and on-the-job training. Four years later, he was promoted to detective.

Detective Henwood was born in a small town in Iowa. He attended the University of Colorado where he obtained his bachelor's in criminal justice. There, he met his wife. He followed her to her hometown. He applied to and was accepted in the police academy where he graduated with top marks. He and his wife have two children, ages four and two.

Nick studied the picture provided with the dossier. Detective Henwood was 6'4" and 210 pounds. He had a flattop haircut and very blond hair, bordering on white. He had a broad face, square jaw, and a thin, long nose. He was clean-shaven with a wide toothy smile. His teeth were almost as white as his hair. Pete had made a note on the printout of the file for Detective Henwood, "The gun used to murder Morgan Wood was from a narcotics case but not one of Detective Henwood's." Nick flipped through a few pages of cases Detective Henwood had worked on, but no names or places immediately stood out to Nick.

He moved on to the next file, Officer Penny Ambrose. Officer Ambrose, thirty-six, was an evidence specialist in central storage. She was responsible for managing chain of custody documentation for all incoming and outgoing evidence. She also maintained the records of stored evidence and was involved in the processing and destruction of evidence no longer required to be held either due to the statutory holding period lapsing or dismissal of a case. She performed her job efficiently and proficiently. She was punctual and well-liked by other members of her team though she was noted to be distant from her colleague and did not socialize outside work.

Six years ago, Officer Ambrose was demoted to officer from corporal. She had been an excellent field officer and was on her way to making sergeant when an unfortunate incident derailed her career. Having taken down a much larger and heavily intoxicated subject, she was struggling to place restraints on said subject when her sergeant arrived and assisted. The subject was struck in the face and rib before being cuffed. After an inquiry and trial by jury, Corporal Ambrose was found to be negligent in her duties as she allowed a detained subject to be injured by use of force, and she was also found negligent as she misrepresented the facts to the initial investigators who, due to bystander video, were able to disprove her affidavit.

After a six-month suspension, she returned with a reduced rank and was given her choice of nonpublic facing clerical positions. A review board may reinstate her to fieldwork after ten years if they feel she was able to execute her duties and uphold the sanctity of her badge. Officer Ambrose was a local, born in the city. She was raised by her father after her mother's untimely death shortly after her second birthday. Her father worked as a carpenter. Officer Ambrose attended the local community college and obtained an associate's degree in criminal studies. She had a black belt in judo and studied Krav Maga. She was an expert marksman with pistol and rifle. Her hobbies included distance cycling and combat sport shooting. She was single and had a dog, a border collie named Harold.

Nick picked up her picture. She had jet-black hair pulled back tightly. Her eyes were dark brown. She had a full, round face and a short, broad nose. She was 5'6" and 175 pounds. She was left-handed. Nick looked at the picture closely, convinced he had seen her before. He could not remember where. Pete wrote a note on Officer Ambrose's file as well, "Under IA investigation due to a missing weapon but not exclusively. Any evidence specialist with access to the weapons to be destroyed cache is being questioned. There's over a dozen names on the list. My sources tell me she is coming up clean from the IA investigation though it is still ongoing."

Nick moved on to the final dossier—Victor "Mack" MacArthur. He was terminated six years ago after an incident in which he kicked a subdued though not yet cuffed suspect. After an inquiry and trial by jury, Sergeant MacArthur was found guilty of assault and battery. However, given his years of service, the judge ordered a twenty-five-thousand-dollar fine and three years of probation. The police department terminated his employment, and he lost his pension. At the time, Mack was fifty years old and a twenty-five-year veteran of the force. Sergeant MacArthur was born in a suburb of the city. He was a star football player in high school. He married his high school sweetheart and took a job in a mill working alongside his father. When the mill shut down, he applied to and was accepted by the police academy. He was well-liked by his fellow officers but had a reputation in the third ward for being a tough cop who was particularly hard on minority members of the community. He had been written up multiple times for excessive use of force but never formally reprimanded. There were rumors he would abuse prisoners in his custody, and on one occasion, the camera into the holding cell went out for ten minutes before an ambulance was requested for an injured prisoner. However, not enough evidence had ever been presented to take any investigation in Mack very far.

In addition to lack of evidence, his fellow officers always stood by his side, never crossing the blue line to report anything about Mack that would support claims of abuse. He was also cited five times for bravery, including once for heroism above and beyond when he dragged an injured officer out of harm's way while under fire.

After losing his job and pension, it was rumored that Mack went into business as a PI and private security officer. Late nights and an irregular schedule strained his marriage. Three years after the loss of his job, Mack divorced his wife. Mack was known to take work where he could get it. A disgraced ex–police sergeant could get work, lots of it, just not with the most reputable of employers.

Nick paged through a few handwritten sheets from Pete. Apparently, Mack called in favors over the years to get help with his cases, and Pete provided the names of as many of those officers as possible. None stood out to Nick. Nick looked at an old photo of Mack. He had a regular taper cut and salt-and-pepper hair. He had a dark-brown neatly trimmed mustache. He had green eyes, a long broad nose, and bushy eyebrows. He had prominent ears, a cleft chin, and—Nick pulled a magnifying glass out—a scar on his left cheek. Nick though that this was the man whom he saw talking with Sarah Honor, but he couldn't be sure. *What would he be doing with Sarah?* Nick thought.

It was getting late, but at this time of year, Nick needed less and less sleep. The more he worked, the more awake he felt. As the Christmas season took full flight, so did Nick's spirit. He paused and found an all-night pizza joint on the local college campus that would deliver. He ordered a large meat lover's pie and stepped outside to wait for it. He brought along his pipe, a relic from days gone by. He clenched the cold clay stem between his teeth. He breathed deep. He held the bowl in his hands, tapping the stem to his lip. Nick had given up smoking his pipe some decades back, not for health reasons but because pipes had gone out of vogue, at least for tobacco. Any number of shops near where his pie was being prepared sold a rainbow of glass pipes for "tobacco use only," but Nick knew better. No, tobacco pipes had gone away, by and large. But still, when he needed to think or clear his thoughts, his pipe was a good distraction for his idle hands.

An hour later, Nick was two slices into his late-night dinner. He found a bottle of soda in the small fridge he kept in the closet, next to some putrefied lo mein. With his belly full and mind clear, Nick returned to his files. He pulled out the autopsy report of Michael Honor Jr. This was not the first such report Nick had read. In fact, he'd read quite a few in his career as an investigator. He briefly thought of the first time he read an autopsy report. The medical science was far less advanced than the report he was currently holding. Much less information was available, and much more speculation was present. Autopsy then was still as much about art as it was about science.

He laughed thinking about how little he knew of human anatomy and physiology then. Biology hadn't been a science, per say, when he was young. And, unlike tonight, anything new or unfamiliar, which, at the time, was everything, couldn't be pulled up with a few keystrokes in a search engine. Nick had spent hours and days, weeks even, at the library learning the basics before moving on to the advanced and finally having some understanding of the report he was reading.

He'd come a long way since then. He had read and reread as much as he possibly could about forensic pathology. He had a decent library at home, full of reference materials, that he'd long ago traded in for subscriptions to the leading journals on the subject which he could access from any Web-enabled device.

After reading through the report, he took a pause. Unlike most of the reports he'd read in his life, this one was notable for only two reasons. One, it was exceedingly brief. Having been performed by a hospital pathologist at the request of the family, there was not the level of detail Nick was used to when reading through a coroner's forensic pathology report. The second remarkable thing was just how unremarkable the report was. The cause of death was simply listed as natural causes related to aging. Nick found this lack of specificity to be exceedingly irritating.

Clearly, one gets old and dies, Nick thought. *But something had to give, right? His heart or kidneys? Anything?* Nick reread the report and again found nothing significant in the findings. The brain, heart, lungs, liver, kidneys, spleen, pancreas, and intestines were all essentially normal, save for the age-related changes that were expected. Nick pulled up one of the journal databases he had access to and read some into this frustrating lack of findings. Nick, someone who frequently looked into suspicious deaths or outright homicides, always found something in the autopsy report. It may not be significant, but there was always something. He had never encountered the autopsy report of an essentially healthy man before. To his astonishment, Nick learned that autopsies in the older population were less frequently performed and that a cause of death was only found in about 70 percent of cases.

Nick put the report away in his safe. He stood and stretched. From his window, he could see the first hint of dawn light breaking over the horizon. Though he hadn't slept in almost twenty-four hours, Nick felt awake and alert. He grabbed his coat and hat and headed out the door. He had found more questions than answers in the last day. It was time he started to get some answers and close this case before it got any more complicated.

Chapter 20

Nick took his papers and coffee in the driver's seat of his car. He had walked in the predawn light and calm of the city, thinking through his next steps. After an hour's contemplation, Nick got a cup of coffee to go along with his preferred papers from the local newsstand. As the sun broke over the horizon and ushered in a beautiful dawn, Nick walked to his car and headed for the wharf.

He pulled into the parking lot of M. Phinck Transportation, pulled out his papers, and began to read. M. Phinck Transportation was a moderate-sized river shipping operation. They would oversee a fleet of three pusher boats: the *Silver Belle*, the *Wonderland*, and the *Feliz Navigacion*. These towboats, square of bow and shallow of draft, were the workhorses of river transport. Each could push up to fifteen barges or 22,500 tons of material. They could transport anything from coal to petroleum to agricultural products. About ten years ago, Michael Jr. bought out M. Phinck and a few other barge companies in an effort to fully vertically integrate his supply chain under the Gabriel Industries umbrella. Shipping by barge was one of the most economical ways to move large quantities from suppliers to factories. They moved corn, soy, high fructose corn syrup, wheat, nuts—anything that didn't require refrigeration.

As an incentive to sell his company, the owner was awarded shares in the company and a board seat to ensure he had a voice in any future decisions that could affect his interests. For Michael Jr., this not only allowed him to streamline services and cut costs by owning a large part of his supply chain, but these barges also moved more than just his goods. They moved wheat upstream from the heartland farms and then turned around to ship coal or wet oil back down river to power plants and cracker facilities. He saved on one leg of the trip and made money on the other. He had made many purchases with these dual benefits over the years, buying out the owners of trucking companies to save money delivering his raw goods to the factory and finished goods to the stores. These same trucks could also make money delivering goods unrelated to the Honor Family cookie business.

Once he owned trucking companies, Michael Jr. naturally moved to owning gas and oil interests. The list of different companies went on and on. In some, but not all cases, board seats and stock were awarded as part of the deal. But only in a few cases were the board seats permanent and seat appointment untouchable. These types of untouchable seats were generally reserved for investors who would not part with their money easily and without whose financial backing none of these other acquisitions could be made. Without the acquisitions, there could be no growth from regional cookie business into a global industrial powerhouse.

M. Phinck was the first river barge acquisition. They were a medium-sized company that had been financially struggling. Michael Jr. had stepped in with a rescue buyout and had offered generous compensation to Mike Phinck for his company. His seat on the board had become the proxy vote for all additional river barge acquisitions, effectively making Mike Phinck the representative for bargemen at the company. A bargeman had a seat at the table, and they, the owners of subsequent river transport companies, could be assured that they would always have a voice at the top. But the fine print on this deal for Mike Phinck was that the chairman could dismiss his seat at will and replace him with an acceptable alternative, that was to say, anyone the chairman wanted to appoint. This had never happened in the past, and only a handful of seats had this total lack of agency. Typically, this provision was reserved for small and inexperienced business owners such as Mike Phinck who signed this type of a deal, not really understanding its meaning. A more typical deal would allow the chairman to dismiss any board member, but the company they represented retained the power to appoint a replacement of their choosing. In total, only four seats, comprising 8 percent of the vote on the board, had seats with these clauses.

Rumor had it, these four seats were replaced by Joseph Honor in August 2018. Nick was hoping to find out if the rumor was true and, if so, why they had been replaced. According to the port schedule, the *Silver Belle*, captained by Mike Phinck, was due in this morning, carrying twenty-two thousand tons of flour bound for the Honor Family Bakery. It was ten thirty, and Nick was finishing with *The Times*. The markets, he read, were up due to good Black Friday numbers. Seasonal flu numbers were up as well, possibly for the same reason. Ugly sweaters were now the most popular commercial piece of holiday clothing.

He rubbed the bridge of his nose and his eyes. The lack of sleep was starting to catch up to him as he had spent the last few hours sedate in a warm car reading the fine print of a newspaper. He got out of his car and paced in the morning chill, the sun just now peaking above the hills and shining light down into the river valley. Steam rolled off the water as the sun warmed the air above it. Nick was suddenly aware of something big moving nearby. Turning to the water, he saw fourteen barges coming into view. The hum of the *Silver Belle*'s five-thousand-horsepower motor churning against the current could be felt more than heard. An hour later, she was tied off, and the ground crew had started the process of unloading the raw flour into nearby train cars for the final leg of the journey. They would be pulled directly into the Honor Family Bakery.

Nick waited patiently as the crew disembarked and, one by one, headed for home in their cars. One man, presumably Captain Phinck, stayed behind. There was no receptionist or other office staff to speak of; the day-to-day operations people were consolidated and moved to an office downtown in one of the many Gabriel Industries office buildings. This office was for the crew to handle on the water business that couldn't be done from the remove of downtown. Bills of lading, crew manifests, and safety documentation all had to be kept close at hand and on the jobsite.

Nick rang the bell by the door. He waited a few minutes and was preparing to ring again when he heard footsteps on the other side of the door. He heard a key being inserted into a lock and a heavy dead bolt turning. The door opened, and a man of about fifty stood in the darkened entryway. He was wearing a bright-yellow watch cap over his close-cropped brown hair. His face was weathered, the skin dark brown from long exposure to the sun and wind. He had a long-sleeve T-shirt of the same OSHA approved yellow under his down vest. He had reading glasses hanging from a lanyard around his neck. His jeans were well-worn, and he had on heavy steel-toed boots. Nick could smell tobacco smoke and beer.

"Can I help you?" the man asked.

"I hope so. I am looking for Mike Phinck. Is he in?"

"Depends. Who are you?"

"I'm Nick Saint, a private investigator. I'm looking into a case that may involve Joseph Honor. I was hoping to speak with Mike." Nick was fairly certain he was already speaking with Mike.

"What kind of case?" the man asked.

"I have a client who may have been wrongly accused of a crime, and I think Joseph may be responsible for setting him up."

The man paused and thought about this for a moment. He pulled a pack of cigarettes from his vest pocket and offered one to Nick, who declined. He lit his cigarette and took a long drag. "I thought you PIs all smoked. That must just be in the movies." He turned and walked into the darkened corridor, motioning for Nick to follow.

A minute later, they were in a cluttered office. Paperwork filled most available surfaces. Nick took a seat on a dusty folding chair.

The man sat behind the desk. He tapped the ash from his cigarette into an overflowing ashtray. "That half-wit Joe couldn't be your guy. Pin a crime on someone else? He's barely able to take care of himself. Hell, without all the paid help, I doubt he could take care of himself." The man put his feet up on the desk and reclined in his chair.

"I take it you are Mike Phinck then?" Nick asked.

"Nothing gets by you, Private I, does it?"

"Your doubts about Joe aside, I'd still like to ask you a few questions."

"What's in it for me? I've been up all night piloting that pusher out there. I've got a ton of other work to do."

Nick replied, "If you weren't interested in talking, why'd you invite me in?"

"It's not every day you get to talk with Santa Claus, now is it, Nick Saint?" He smiled, and Nick scowled.

"Do I look like a jolly fat man in a red suit?"

Mike laughed. "No, you look like a grumpy asshole in an old suit."

Nick laughed. "Thank you."

"Truth is," Mike replied, "I've read a few articles about you in *The Post*, crimes you solved. People seem to really think you're a right jolly old elf."

"What do you think?" Nick asked.

"I think, Santa or not, it can't hurt to ask what's in it for me."

Nick rubbed his temple. "Anything in particular you'd like? Footballs are popular this year."

Mike put his feet down and sat forward in his chair. "My board seat, I want it back."

"Oh, is that all?"

"If it's not too much to ask."

"Alright. You answer my questions, and I'll see what I can do about your board seat." Nick pulled a notebook out of his pocket and marked down, "Mike Phinck—board seat." He put the notebook back in his pocket.

"What was that you were writing down?"

"It's just my list. Do we have a deal?"

Mike laughed. "Just don't forget to check it twice. Okay. It's a deal. Ask away." Mike leaned back into his chair.

"You've already answered one of my questions. You were a board member at Gabriel Industries, and you were let go by Joseph Honor."

"That is correct." Mike lit another cigarette and opened a can of warm beer. He offered one to Nick, but he declined.

"When were you let go?"

"August, this year."

"Why were you let go?"

"Joseph was trying to solidify his position. He called an emergency board meeting just before our regular meeting. He said he had a big announcement. When the meeting started, he announced that myself and three other board members were being dismissed and replaced. To represent the bargemen, he named my rival in the business. Technically, we all work for the same company now, but there's a fairly complicated bonus structure built into our contracts with Gabriel Industries. Short version, the company that moves the most tonnage gets a huge payout at the end of the year."

Nick interrupted, "Is that why you're out on the water?"

"Yes and no. With an extra pilot, we can push through more tonnage. There's rules on the amount of time we can operate, kind of like airline pilots. But back to your question, that's not the only reason I'm out there. Bonus or not, I was born into this work. My father started this company. I was named after him though I'm not a junior. I grew up around the water. I love the work. I'll never give it up." He paused to take a drink.

Nick picked up, "And he wanted new blood on the board? Any idea why?"

"It was no secret we were voting to remove him and take the company public. We were headed that way once Michael Jr. got sick. A lot of the board is only out to make money. When Michael Jr. got sick, they were like sharks that smelled blood in the water. They'd been waiting for an opportunity to get the Honor family out and go public, but a few of us were pretty loyal to Michael. My business was struggling before he came around. Rail and truck have taken a lot of our business, and coal use is down. I'm all for clean energy, but coal was my bread and butter. Michael found a way to keep me running, and I was making good money."

Mike rose and paced back and forth behind his desk as he told his story. "Those of us loyal to Michael had hope he'd recover, but after a few months, word leaked that he had Alzheimer's or something similar. He wasn't coming back. I've never been keen on Joseph. For a while, he oversaw transport—truck, barge, rail, the company fleet.

It was a shit show. Michael pulled him, but the damage was done. When it looked like Joseph was going to take over, I decided going public was in my best interest. Unfortunately, Michael died before we could go public. Joseph took control, and we were stuck with him. We could move against him right away but—"

Nick broke in, "He had the majority vote. He could block any action."

"Well, he did have the largest share, but it wasn't a majority. Michael and his kids owned 51 percent of the company, but the kids didn't have voting seats on the board. Michael had, and now Joseph has a 47 percent vote on the board. We could have voted him out if the board unanimously voted against him. We could have pushed him out."

"So why didn't you?"

"At first, we didn't have the votes. A few percent of the votes are dear family friends, and they wouldn't budge. They wanted to give the kid a chance. When Michael was sick and had no vote, those few votes didn't matter. We could outvote them, but with Michael's 47 percent back at the table in the hands of Joseph, we needed every single board member to vote together against Joseph, or it was a moot point."

"So what changed? Why'd they suddenly decide to vote him out?" Nick asked.

"In June, Joseph got hit with a perfect shitstorm. He made a particularly bad call involving the purchase of commodities and cost the company millions. When the news broke, he was so distraught, he went on a bender. He was caught, well, it doesn't matter what he was caught doing. It was enough to turn the few hold outvotes against him. We were prepared to take him out in August, but then one of our members who represented about 10 percent of the vote backed out. She said she needed time to think. Then Joseph called his emergency meeting, and an additional 4 percent of the vote went to him when he dumped the four nonpermanent board members, myself among them, and replaced them with allies."

"Couldn't they turn on him too? Vote him out?" Nick asked.

"Sure, why not? And even with 51 percent of the vote with his new board members, his incompetence could sink him. The rest of the board could take him to court, prove he's costing them and the company money. They could claim damages from his poor leadership and win a huge sum of money or ask that he be removed and the company be allowed to go public. The board could appoint a new CEO and chairman of the board."

Nick thought about this for a while. Mike broke the silence. "Bottom line, Joe is out. It's a matter of when and how now, not if. If his new board members hold on to his side, it'll be a legal battle but one he'll lose. I'm sure of that. Or the board turns those four votes, and he loses the board vote."

"What if he appointed a new CEO and chairman of the board?"

"It could work," Mike said. "For a while. It would complicate things for sure. But like I've said, the kid is not that smart. And I think he likes the power. He'll fight to the end."

"Which board member waffled?" Nick asked.

"June Dawson, an older lady. She invested a decent chunk of change in the '80s, I think. Anyway she's been on the board for a long time and is very influential, not just her vote share but her personality. She can swing a vote when she needs to."

"So she's a brilliant orator?" Nick asked.

"I'd say she's more of a stonehearted bitch," Mike replied.

"Right," Nick said. "One last question, have you ever heard of Stephen Dash?"

"The Dasher of Dreams guy?"

"Yeah, him," Nick replied.

"Well, I've read about him in the paper. Real piece of work, stealing from kids. And at Christmas!"

"Thanks for your time, Mike." Nick shook Mike's hand and started for the exit.

Mike followed. He stopped Nick at the door. "You won't forget our deal, will you?"

"I've made my list," Nick replied as he turned to leave.

Mike closed the door and slammed the dead bolt shut. "Just don't forget to check it twice."

Chapter 21

Stephen Dash woke with a start. He had been reading on his sofa, one of the few pieces of furniture currently in his possession. Holly had left a few hours ago to try and get more of their belongings moved from storage to their home. The police and the district attorney, satisfied that all the necessary evidence had been obtained, released the Dash's belongings back to them. They were free to move their belongings from storage to their new home. The storage unit, having been paid up front for six months, was currently not an issue. However, most of their funds had been frozen by the district attorney and weren't likely to be freed anytime soon. Getting a moving van or a moving company without money was out of the question. Family and friends, while sympathetic, seemed perpetually busy whenever Holly asked for assistance. Stephen was confined to their home on house arrest until trial so, while willing, could not be of any use. Holly had taken to loading as many useful items as she could into her car and driving them to their new home. This took most of the day as she couldn't fit a whole box of dishes into her car but could take select dishes in a smaller box. She had spent her last few days finding necessary items such as dishes and cooking utensils, unpacking them from large moving boxes, and then repacking into smaller boxes that she could transport in her car. She would be able to load her car with the few boxes it could hold and drive home.

Stephen—with no TV, no job, no Internet, and, for the last few days, no company—had been reading the few books Holly found and brought home. It was while rereading *The Count of Monte Cristo* that he had fallen asleep. Now he was suddenly and widely awake. The sound of the doorbell now mixed with persistent and loud knocking. He rose from the couch but hesitated when he reached the hallway to the front door. Could he be sure, with everything going on, that he should answer the door? He thought for a moment about all the terrible what-ifs he could imagine. As his mind raced from thoughts of being arrested again to being accosted by journalists to being assaulted or worse by those who had set him up, he heard a familiar voice yell, "I know you're in there! They won't let you leave. You're on house arrest. Open the door, the groceries are getting warm."

Stephen opened the door for Nick, who was holding a few plastic bags with the logo of the local market. "It's starting to rain too," Nick said. "Get the rest out of the trunk, will ya?" Nick pushed past Stephen and down the hallway to the kitchen.

The two put away the groceries in near silence, only speaking when Nick wanted to know where to put the sugar or the cereal. Afterward, Nick poured a glass of water from the tap. "I can't thank you enough for the groceries. We've been trying to be conservative with our shopping since our money isn't liquid at the moment. We've been relying on the generosity of family and friends, but…well, innocent until proven guilty may work for the courts—"

Nick interrupted, "But doesn't apply to public opinion. I know. But don't thank me too much. Your contract says I get reimbursed for incidentals." Nick winked.

Stephen laughed. "So you came all this way to buy me groceries and to let me know I'll owe you for them?"

"Not really. This was an afterthought. No, I came here to find out about the Little Drummer Boy audit."

"Okay, what do you want to know?"

"Why was there an audit called for? Who initiated the audit?"

"That's a good question. I don't know."

"You're the treasurer. How do you not know why you were audited?" Nick asked.

"Oh, I know the why. You asked about the who. I guess we—and by we, I mean the board of directors—called for the audit to be conducted by an outside auditor."

"So you were in favor of an audit?" Nick asked.

"Of course! Why wouldn't I have been? I had nothing to hide," Stephen said.

"And the police and the DA, they know this?"

"I'm assuming so. They have all the records from the Little Drummer Boy. They can read the minutes from our board meeting where we voted, myself included, to have an audit."

Nick stroked his chin. "And this doesn't seem odd to them?"

"I guess not. Honestly, I think they'll rationalize every move I made. Why vote to approve an audit? Because I'm hoping I covered up my theft from the auditors. If I voted against the audit, it would look like I had something to hide. There's definitely a way to spin my decisions to a jury, Nick."

Nick considered this. "Okay, let's leave the obvious aside. You and the board called for it. Why? Why did you call for an audit right before the money went missing?"

"We didn't, not right before," Stephen replied.

"So when did you call for it then?" Nick asked.

"It was at our March quarterly board meeting. It takes time to set up an audit. You have to hire an outside auditor, and then you have to get all your paperwork prepped and ready to hand over to the auditor. It can take months to get ready."

"So you'd been working on this for a few months?"

"I had been, which is why the whole panicked call from Morgan, his disappearance, and the missing money was all a shock. One minute, everything is fine, and the next? Well, I'm stuck being called a thief."

"Why did you call for the audit, Stephen?" Nick pressed.

"Well, I didn't, not personally. I wasn't against it though. I trust, well, trusted Morgan, so an audit should've been easy. The board, as a whole, agreed to call for an audit, but it wasn't our idea either. We got a letter saying that a very wealthy donor wanted to endow our charity with a huge sum of money. Who the donor is or was, I can't say. None of us can. They expressed concern, maybe not concern. They expressed the desire for transparency. Essentially, they wanted us to open our books to someone independent. If the audit said we were clean and handling the money as advertised, then the donor would move on to the task of actually setting up the endowment."

"So you get a random letter that could be from anyone that says to open your books, and they'll give you a huge fortune. Doesn't that sound odd to you? I mean, what incentive did you have to go through all that work to audit the Little Drummer Boy?" Nick asked.

"One hundred thousand dollars was the incentive. We were given one hundred thousand dollars with no strings attached."

"Okay," Nick said. "So you got one hundred thousand dollars to audit your books. That money can be traced, right? I'm assuming you didn't find a briefcase full of money with the letter. One hundred thousand dollars is a lot of money. Someone has to know where it came from, right?"

"No, there wasn't a briefcase full of money, and no, it can't be traced."

"I'm lost. It's not cash, so it was a check or a banknote. An electronic transfer? Someone should be able to track this money."

"Have you heard of Bitcoin, Nick?"

"Yes, well, maybe? It's a digital currency, right?"

"Yes, it's complicated how it works, but the end result is you have verifiable but untraceable funds. It's part of its allure. No central bank. No governmental control. It's a free market currency. And we accepted one hundred thousand in Bitcoin, which we exchanged for US dollars right away. And then we started the audit process."

"But one hundred thousand is a large sum of money. If I had a person whom I thought was your anonymous donor, I could look through bank records or something and see the Bitcoin purchase or, barring that, a corresponding loss of one hundred thousand dollars, right?"

"In theory, yes. What's this all about, Nick? Do you think it's the donor the one who set me up?"

Nick paced through the living room, arms crossed behind his back. He didn't speak for a few minutes. He was thinking through the possibilities raised by this information. Finally, he uncrossed his arm and stopped to look at Stephen. "It's definitely a possibility. If a big money donor was interested in the Little Drummer Boy, why go through the trouble of being so secretive?"

Stephen said, "It's not uncommon. If you don't want people constantly asking for more money, then you go through some intermediary."

"Point taken," Nick said. Then he continued, "So this might just be someone who legit wants to give away a fortune to the Little Drummer Boy, and whoever set you up just glommed onto the audit and used it against you. But the donor could also have been behind this to set you up."

"Yeah," Stephen said, "but to what end, Nick? What did I do to anyone?"

"Not sure yet. But you are one of Michael Honor Jr.'s sons, and he wanted to bring you in. Your brother—"

"Half brother," Stephen corrected.

"Your half brother is fighting to keep the company private and family owned. The board is trying to take the company public and drop Joseph and the family from the family business. Someone must've figured your relationship out and is trying to keep you out of the picture."

"Okay, Nick, but who?" Stephen asked.

"That's the hundred-thousand-dollar question, isn't it?" Nick said.

Chapter 22

The Sussex House sat high on a hill, about ten miles outside town. From its vantage, a visitor could look down the river valley to the city below. The Sussex House was the main building on a sprawling four-hundred-acre campus that was known as the Sussex Club. The club was constructed at the turn of the twentieth century as an escape from the heat and stench of the city below. The city's elite industrialists, bankers, financiers, and the well-connected political class envisioned an enclave outside the city but within easy reach, where they could meet to discuss politics, business, science, art, and literature. Membership allowed the wives of these well-to-do men to take tea on Fridays and discuss whatever it was women were wont to discuss. It came as a surprise to the same men when the Friday tea became a hotbed of suffragette activity. Women of influence used their connections to push for the passage of the Nineteenth Amendment. Having cleared that hurdle in 1920, these same women began working on other pressing social issues, the first being the inclusion of women as full and equal members in the Sussex Club. By 1960, independent women of means and influence were availing themselves of the club and all its amenities as full and equal members.

Unlike many private clubs of the time and of today, the Sussex Club was not built around golf. In fact, the members eschewed the norm and had no interest in golf whatsoever. Instead, they placed their considerable wealth into creating sprawling gardens, redolent with birdsong and the smell of flowers in the summer and filled with the scent of pine and soft light in the winter. Modeled after the gardens of English estates, members were free to wander, sit, read, and, now as a family-friendly club, play with their children in an idyllic setting just a short drive from the city.

The majority of the four hundred acres was preserved as a place of natural beauty, free from the meticulous grooming necessary to create the cultivated English gardens that surround Sussex House. A team of arborists and horticulturists worked to ensure a lasting sense of natural splendor along miles of walking trails, many of which afford breathtaking views of the river valley below. These large swaths of nature also served as a barrier between "the world" and "the club," limiting access to the main grounds and affording the elite privacy from prying eyes.

Though a relatively short drive from the city, visitors felt like they left their world and entered into the English countryside. Driving parallel to the river along an historic highway that was once the main thoroughfare out of the city, one turned off the historic highway onto a winding road that cut around the hillside through increasingly sparse housing before turning onto a small private drive that dived into a thick wood.

Past the thick stand of trees that separated the grounds from the main road, the road passed by a brick gatehouse and under a grand-arched gateway into a well-tended but natural appearing meadow, surrounded by stands of old growth trees. Paths meandered through the meadow to benches and gazebos. Leaving the meadow, one would once again pass through a dense wood. Breaking out of the wood and topping a small rise, the Sussex House came into view. Georgian in style, echoing the country estates of England, the house was constructed of red brick and white sandstone on the corners. It rose to three stories high, each wide level had eight tall and unadorned windows, four on each side of the house, the symmetry providing a simple yet elegant look. The house had a grand-pillared portico entry with marbled steps that was the visual and physical center of the house. The road wound past the grand front entryway where, in days gone by, drivers would leave their passengers before continuing to the stables that were later razed to build the parking lot which was cleverly hidden behind a small rise off to the side of the house. In the modern era of the club, the road had been modified with a Y intersection at the side of the house with one branch leading to the parking lot and the other circling around to a covered carport with valet.

In opposition to the plain exterior of the building, the interior was opulent with marbled floors, decadent wallpaper, crystal chandeliers, large working fireplaces, wood-paneled libraries with collections of books to rival most public libraries, leather armchairs, Tiffany lamps, formal dining rooms, a grand ballroom, two English-style pubs, and a smoking lounge. There was a collection of fine art donated by the founders of the club hung throughout the halls and sitting rooms. The collection was preserved and curated by the city art museum in exchange for triannual public exhibitions of the works.

Despite the modernization of the club, especially its charter and rules, many old traditions persisted. The ladies Friday tea was still observed every week with exceptions for holidays. It was now where the women of power, influence, and means come to meet and network, free from the distractions of "the mediocre men of privilege" with whom they compete. And, as unlikely as it seemed, Nick was, this Friday afternoon, on his way to tea with the ladies of the Sussex Club or, specifically, one lady in particular, June Dawson. He wasn't sure of her connection, if any, to the case, but she hesitated taking Gabriel Industries public without any warning. And, Nick found, she was very active and heavily invested in the cryptocurrency community.

It had been a while since his last visit to the Sussex House, and seeing it came into view as he crested the hill still filled him with awe. It was a truly beautiful building, and the panorama of the last falling leaves, river valley, and city in the distance was a sight to behold. Nick entered the Wells Lounge and left his hat and coat at the checkroom. He made his way through the gathering crowd at the bar. Finding a staff member near the door, he asked, "Where might I find the ladies tea?"

The staff member, taken aback, replied, "It's in the Uppark Room, but it's the ladies tea, sir."

"I understand," Nick said. "I'll only be a minute. I have urgent business with one of the members. I promise, I'll only take a minute." Nick then leaned in and whispered to the staff member, asking that he should have the manager take a close look at the membership section of the club charter. And with that, Nick headed up the stairs to the second floor, the Uppark Room being central to the house with a balcony overlooking the gardens.

He entered, scanning each table, looking for June Dawson, having found her picture on the Gabriel Industries board of directors website. June Dawson, seventy-seven, was the daughter and only child of Samuel Dawson. Samuel Dawson was the heir to Dawson Steelworks and the associated family fortune. A lifetime of tobacco use had led to his early death at the age of forty-four. June's mother assumed control of the family fortune and nominally Dawson Steelworks though the board of directors preferred a man to take control and a CEO, so a board seat was appointed to oversee the company for June's mother, Louise.

Growing up in the shadow of men deciding what was best for her mother, June determined at a young age that she would be her own woman and lead the life she wanted. She attended Harvard, where she obtained a degree in business, followed by her Juris Doctorate, also from Harvard. Having no interest in actually practicing law, June, at the age of twenty-eight, took control of Dawson Steelworks and the family fortune. Her knowledge of business and the law allowed her to take back control from those who had shut her mother out.

Unfortunately, a few years after retaking her family fortune and business, the bottom fell out of the American steel industry. Dawson Steelworks was forced to close and at a considerable loss to June's wealth. Undeterred, she took her remaining capital and began aggressively investing. The Honor Family Bakery and later Gabriel Industries were profitable investments though not her only investment. By her fiftieth birthday, she was one of the one hundred wealthiest Americans and in the top 50 wealthiest women in the world.

Nick spotted her seated at a table, front and center by the window, looking nearly identical to her publicity photos, her silver hair cut in an ear-length bob. She wore oversize tortoise shell glasses that sat high upon her aquiline nose. She wore a cream-colored sweater with a matching floor-length skirt and shawl and a multistring pearl necklace with matching bracelets.

Nick crossed the floor toward her and noticed she was not seated alone. Seated in a wheelchair opposite June was a woman of about seventy years. She had a slight droop to the right side of her face and sat in a way that favored her right side. A well-dressed attendant was by her side. Judging by her demeanor and her attentiveness to this woman, she was likely a hired help and not family. As he got closer, he couldn't help but think this woman resembled...his thought was interrupted. "Nick Saint? Is that you?"

Nick looked up to see Sarah Honor approaching the same table. "It is, Ms. Honor. I didn't take you for the 'ladies Friday tea' type."

They shook hands, and Sarah sat at June's table. "I'm not really," Sarah said once comfortably seated. "But my mother"—she motioned to the woman in the wheelchair—"was or is, I suppose."

The woman made no movement at the mention of her. June Dawson, however, did. "Sarah, don't speak of your mother in the past tense, especially as she is right there, dear."

"You're right, June. Mr. Saint, my mother was a regular at tea until her stroke. She's not able to take tea herself, but with me in tow, she still comes to visit. She has always loved the gardens in warm weather and, in colder weather, the conservatory. We used to walk there together around Christmas. She loved it so much that Father had one built just like it at home for her. He filled it with morning glories, her favorite. Did you know there are hundreds of different types of morning glories? Mother did. She had reds and blues, deep purples. It was her oasis at home, but she still loved to come here and walk among the flowers, especially at Christmas. Even though she can't stroll like she used to, I believe it is good for her spirits to still come here and be among friends, see the gardens and her beloved conservatory."

"There you go again, dear, speaking as though she's not here. And Sarah has taken on her mother's social duties for the family, making the rounds, speaking with the most powerful women in town."

June turned her gaze to Nick but continued speaking to Sarah. "I don't believe we've been introduced."

Nick extended his hand and began to speak but was cut off by Sarah, "Ms. June Dawson, may I introduce Mr. Nick Saint, private investigator."

June extended her hand for a polite and formal handshake while remaining seated. "Might you be the same Nick Saint who rescued our dear Sarah the other evening from a rather, shall we say, delicate situation?"

"I don't know if I'd call it a rescue as such, Ms. Dawson. I just happened to show up at the right time," Nick replied.

"Come now, from what Sarah told me, without your convenient arrival, she may have had some real trouble with—"

Sarah broke in, "An upset actor, June."

"That's right. Yes, thespians can be so, well, dramatic." June smiled wryly at this.

"Oh, ho, ho, yes, quite true." Nick laughed.

June looked at Sarah just briefly and then back to Nick. "Well, Mr. Saint, I don't believe Ms. Honor needs any rescue today, and as you can see, you're causing a bit of a stir as you are, I'm afraid, a thorn among the roses."

Nick looked around, but the room, as a whole, seemed completely unaware of his presence. "Well, I promise to be brief, Ms. Dawson. May I sit?"

"No, I'd rather you not, Mr. Saint. However brief you believe you may be, I assure you, your stay will be ever much more so." She waved for a server who came quickly. June whispered to the young woman who briskly walked from the room.

"Okay then, June, I'll be brief." Nick dropped all formality and had raised his voice, just enough to actually cause a stir without seeming unhinged. "I have a client who was wrongly accused of a crime. I have evidence to show he had been targeted to take the fall for said a crime. Further, I have proof that those who planted the fraudulent evidence against my client have ties to certain financial interests. And you share those interests, June. These supposed crimes were discovered when a large and anonymous donation was made to a charity utilizing cryptocurrency. This donation triggered a financial audit as it was a requirement of the anonymous donor should the charity wish to receive a large donation from this donor. Just before the audit, the financial records of said charity were edited and data was inserted that made it seem as though my client had been stealing considerable sums of money from the charity. Now, June, since you have financial ties to the middlemen in this conspiracy and have the means and motive for having done so, I came here to ask you directly about your involvement. I had come as a courtesy to allow you a chance to answer some questions and possibly exonerate yourself. However, as I'm certain you sent for the manager to have me thrown out, I am now forced to rather loudly and publicly assert my suspicions and eschew any pretense of civil conversation regarding said suspicions. But I assure you, madam, I'll stay as long as I wish. And I wish to stay until I get some answers." Now all eyes in the room truly were on Nick and June.

June dabbed the corners of her mouth with a napkin and set it upon the table. She stood and squared off with Nick. "I may be old, sir, but I've got a lot of fight in me. You've come here and embarrassed me, accusing me of a crime—"

Nick cut her off, "Do you deny being heavily invested in cryptocurrency?"

"Of course, I don't. It's part of my portfolio, but I don't know much about it. I pay a staff of people to manage my investment."

"And do you deny making a large donation to the Little Drummer Boy with a provision that they perform an audit?"

She paused briefly. "Sir, you are unwelcome here, and I believe it is time you leave." June's gaze broke from Nick's and moved to just over his shoulder.

Nick turned to see the manager approaching, looking less than assured. He approached not Nick, but June. The club manager whispered into June's ear. "That is preposterous!"

"I'm sorry, ma'am, but it's true. He told me to look it up when he arrived. I think he knew this would happen."

Nick smiled the self-assured smile of someone who knew they had the upper hand in an argument. It was the smile of someone who was sure they had won one before their opponent knew they had lost.

"I'm on the membership committee," June began. "I've read all the bylaws, and this man is not part of them. He has no right to be here." Her dignified anger had changed into an outright fury. The ladies tea had shifted from surreptitiously stealing glances at the curiosity taking place at June Dawson's table to blatantly staring at a sight never before seen at tea, at least not in any of their lifetimes. All conversation in the room had stopped, including that of all staff, as all eyes turned to watch what one patron later described as "a truly entertaining spectacle."

The manager opened the club charter to a bookmarked page. "Ma'am, if you'll just read what I have here."

"I've read it all, you simpering fool. There's no mention of Nick Saint in there."

Nick nodded to the manager. "Read it aloud please," Nick said.

The manager read, "Section 12, paragraph 2, all club grounds and rights are afforded to Saint, Nicholas. All members and staff are to allow him to conduct business and are to assist him in said business if at all possible. The discharge of his duties is considered essential and should not be impeded."

"That? You call that proof of his right to be here? Saint Nicholas is a fiction! A myth! A Christmas fairy tale! That was put in there for parents to read to their children before coming to the holiday party. It is a joke, and you know it."

Seeing that the eyes of everyone in the room fixated on her, June continued, "You all know it! The Santa clause was meant as a yuletide joke!"

Her face, reddened by her outburst, turned a shade of purple when Nick laughed. "Oh, ho, ho, ho! You weren't much of a lawyer, were you?"

"What in the hell does that mean?" June asked indignantly.

"Well, to start, the document never mentions Santa Claus. Though many people interchange Santa Claus and Saint Nicholas, legally, in this club's charter, only the latter is mentioned. And there's an important piece of punctuation there that a lawyer should really have picked up on, if they were any good."

June grabbed the book from the manager and began reading to herself. Nick, reciting from memory, spoke the words aloud, "All club grounds and rights are afforded to Saint"—he paused—"comma"—smiled widely—"Nicholas."

To the room, he said, "Nick Saint, pleasure to meet you all." June dropped the book onto the table. Nick strode toward the door, grabbing a tea cake on his way. "Thank you, June, this has been a truly enlightening conversation."

Chapter 23

December arrived with a heavy snow early in the morning. By noon, the sun shone bright as the clouds pushed out to the east. Six inches of fresh snow blanketed the city. Being the weekend, road crews were slow to clean streets, and city residents were even slower still to clear their sidewalks and driveways. Children and adults alike were overjoyed at the prospect of a white Christmas. They laughed in parks and in yards. Snowmen were built. Snowball fights happened. Under a blanket of white, the city felt revitalized and reborn, a fresh white canvas on which to paint a new day.

Nick had watched the snowfall for most of the early morning. The December wind carried not just snow but something very old with it. Nick may have left behind his life as the bringer of yuletide joy, but the spirit still found him this time of year. By midmorning, as the snowfall was slowing, he had laced up his old boots after applying a fresh coat of waterproofing. It was an old home recipe made of tallow, pine resin, and beeswax. He had traded in his light trench coat for a heavier deep forest-green overcoat with fur lining. He had walked the city, taking in the sights and sounds. He breathed air that was fresh and clean, the snow having scrubbed the soot and smog from the air. The snow-covered roads dissuaded, at least temporarily, all but the most determined drivers. It was, in the most literal sense, a breath of fresh air.

Nick had picked up a coffee and bagel and sat in the park, watching children laughing and people passing. He had changed benches a few times after attracting the attention of children who, to their parents' dismay, approached the old and grumpy-looking man in the green coat like moths to a flame. As he headed home, the snowfall having subsided, a curious scent of pine followed him with a strong breeze. Nick had decided it was time to speak with Joseph Honor, and he now knew where to find him.

When Nick left his house later that day, the magic of the morning had left and the old city had returned. The roads had been cleared, and piles of gray-black snow lined the sidewalks. Salt caked the walkways and stairs. The smell of exhaust once again filled the air. "Somehow, the snow that had made the city shine this morning has turned it to shit tonight," Nick grumbled as he cleared off his car. He had kept the heavier winter boots but changed back into his usual lighter coat, better to stay comfortable during a stakeout.

Miraculously, as if by magic, a parking spot opened on the otherwise packed south side of the city. Known for having more bars per block than anywhere else in the state, Saturday night, even after a snowstorm, was the spot for nightlife in the city. Dance clubs, concert venues, hookah bars, college bars, punk bars, strip clubs, greasy spoon diners, and upscale dining were all crowded together, block after block. Joseph Honor, known for his, as his family might say, indiscretions, was a frequent visitor to the night scene along the strip. In particular, he favored a dance club which happened to be across the street from where Nick was parked.

Joseph was known to drink and to enjoy the company of women, usually younger women. He saw himself as the life of the party, spending heavily on expensive bottles of alcohol and sending drinks from said bottles to women whose company he favored. Despite his playboy attitude, Joseph still wanted a modicum of privacy. Though he couldn't keep all his social activities off the Internet and out of the hands of the paparazzi, it didn't mean he wanted to be in the background of a thousand Instagram photos with his arm around a college junior, sipping shots with the club dancers or with his hands on anyone that wasn't his wife. So Joseph, along with others like him, primarily sport stars and the children of the wealthy, tended to frequent a handful of clubs that offered VIP services, such

Nick Saint and the Dasher of Dreams

as private rooms and private booths with dedicated and discrete waitstaff and top-notch security.

Wonderland was just such a club, catering to a higher price clientele in general. And to ensure that those customers spending fifteen dollars on a martini felt it was worth it, Wonderland made sure they all knew there was an even more exclusive area in the back that was frequented by the rich and famous.

Nick tapped the alert on his phone, opening the city parking app. He added another two hours to the virtual meter and locked his screen. *I do love this app,* Nick thought as he remembered how often he used to get out to feed the meter to keep parked in the same spot for a long stakeout. He didn't always feed the meter. On occasion, he had weighed the cost of the meter versus the cost of the ticket and had decided the latter to be cheaper than the former and just let the meter run out.

Tonight was not one of those nights. This particular part of the city was known to have tow trucks patrolling, waiting for the call from the meter reader. Cars parked for more than one hour past their meter expiration were promptly towed. The area thrived on high turnover. Bars and restaurants need a steady stream of customers to keep the cash flowing and in turn, taxes to keep filling the city coffers. Officially, due to the high number of bars, any car that was past its meter by more than an hour was likely to see an intoxicated driver show up and try to drive home. Strict enforcement and towing kept the roads safer, but Nick, who'd been around for a long time, knew better.

Nick had hoped to get to the club before Joseph and catch him on the way in. He preferred a sober interview to an inebriated one, but he'd take what he could get. It seemed the longer the night wore on that this taste of winter had driven Joseph to Wonderland early. Around midnight, Nick saw a flash of light in the alley next to Wonderland. A door had opened briefly, and a lone figure exited. At first, this person stood still as the door closed, then pulled on a hat and gloves. The person was hidden by the dark, and Nick couldn't even make out if it was a man or woman. The person was fishing around in their coat pocket, or so Nick thought, and then there was a small spark of light as they lit a cigarette. At first, Nick took this to be an employee on break. Then the person walked out of the dark and into the light of the club marquee. Nick sprang from the car as Joseph Honor turned out of the alley and began walking down the strip, away from Wonderland.

Nick quickly caught up to Joseph, who was walking slowly and, it would seem, without purpose or a destination. Perhaps he'd left the club for some cold air or to think. Perhaps he was going to let the winds of fate take him where they may.

Nick fell into step next to Joseph and asked, "Joseph Honor?"

He stopped, turned to Nick, and exhaled a lungful of smoke in Nick's direction. "Depends on who's asking."

"Nick Saint, private investigator."

"You're that guy who caused a big row at the Sussex Club, right? My assistant told me about it. You caused a pretty carefully worded apology email to be sent out to the membership."

Nick smiled. "Yeah, that was me."

It was Joseph's turn to smile. "I heard you really tore into June Dawson." Nick nodded, and Joseph continued, "Good. I can't stand that bitch. She and my father were close, but I've never found her to have any redeeming qualities."

"I'm glad you approved," Nick said. "But I'm not here for your approval. I need to ask you a few questions."

Joseph dropped his cigarette butt to the sidewalk and ground it out under the toe of his shoe. He took another out and offered one to Nick. Nick shook his head no and waited while Joseph lit another cigarette and took a long drag.

"Okay," he said, exhaling the smoke, "ask away."

"You called a board meeting in August with the promise of a big announcement. Then you replaced four minor board members. What was your big announcement?"

"You answered your own question. I was replacing four board members." Joseph began walking again, and Nick followed.

"That's not a reason for an emergency board meeting. You could've done that at any time. No meeting necessary. What were you really planning to announce?"

Joseph considered for a moment before answering, "Do you like nature documentaries, Nick? I do. In the animal kingdom, sometimes a smaller animal needs to make itself appear bigger to ward off predators. It works for humans too. If you're being attacked by a wild animal, you make noise and raise your arms up over your head. You appear bigger than you really are."

"So that was all posturing then? You called a meeting, replaced a few board members? To what end? To prove you could? To prove you were not to be messed with?" Nick asked.

"Something like that, yeah." Joseph stopped and turned to Nick. "What's this really about, Nick? I hear you're asking about a charity called Little Drummer Boy, and now you are asking me about a board meeting. Quit beating around the bush and ask what you came to ask."

Nick was surprised and took a minute to collect his thoughts. "Okay then," he said, having recovered. "Tell me about your brother."

"There it is," Joseph said, pointing to Nick with his cigarette. "So you know my secret too."

"What secret is that, Joseph?" Nick asked.

"That I have a half brother that my father kept from me and my sister."

"How did you find out?" Nick asked.

"By accident. When Dad got sick, I started to take over the business, but I had no real authority to do so. I just did it, and no one stopped me. I've got the right name, I guess. When he died…" Joseph's voice quavered, and he stopped to wipe a tear from his eye. Then he continued, "When he died, I took over for real. With that came access to all his files. IT unlocked his computer for me. Anything on it was considered property of the company, and I owned the company. I started to go through his files, trying to piece together what he was doing, what he was planning for the future. His assistant, the COO, VPs, all were very helpful, mind you, but they weren't him. I needed to be him if I wanted to save the company."

"Save it from what?" Nick asked.

"I needed to save it from going public. The board moved quickly while Dad was ill, but I beat them… With Dad gone, I was able to slow things down. I knew they were going to work around me, but I could slow them down. If Dad had anything big in the works, well, maybe I could do something big and turn some votes back my way."

"And your brother?"

"Some guy named Stephen Dash, but I'm betting you knew that."

"I do know it," Nick said.

"Dad had a saved Heritage DNA test result. Stephen is his son. Imagine the shock of finding out from your dead father's computer that he had DNA proof he has another son and that he never told you."

"What else did you find, Joseph?"

There was a long pause. After several minutes, Joseph continued, "I worked my whole life to take over for Dad, and he was just going to replace me with some accident he had?" A tear rolled down his cheek. "I know I'm not perfect, but he didn't even give me a chance."

"Did anyone else know?" Nick asked.

"The shitty thing, Nick, is Dad was right. Even if he gave me a chance, the board was always going to pull away from me. Dad? He was in too strong position. They could never get rid of him. But me? I guess I'll always be just not good enough for anyone."

"And Stephen?" Nick asked.

"Just as shitty as me, I guess. Maybe more so. I'm just lousy to my own kids. He stole from a bunch of orphans."

"Joseph," Nick began but stopped. He was suddenly aware that they were not alone. Someone was watching them. He turned his head slowly from side to side but didn't see anyone besides the usual street traffic. "Joseph, let's walk." Nick started to walk and Joseph followed. "Did anyone else know, Joseph? About Stephen? Did you tell anyone?"

"Outside of the family? No. Nobody I know of."

Nick was now looking for who was watching them, as he was fairly certain they were being followed. About a block after they began walking, he noticed someone in the reflection on a car window. He saw him again a block later in the window of a shop, about ten to twenty paces behind. "When you found out your dad wanting to give the company to your half brother, you were angry. I get it. But why go after him? Why ruin his life? Nobody knew about him. Your father never said anything about him to anyone. Why did you do it?"

Joseph stopped, and Nick stopped beside him, turning so he could see the way they'd just come. The man Nick had noticed kept walking and passed Nick and Joseph. He tried to hide his face, but Nick recognized him immediately, Victor MacArthur. And Nick was sure he was definitely the same man who he saw run from the parking lot encounter with Sarah Honor. Nick watched as he walked out of sight but still felt like he was being watched. Nick thought it must be the other man from the parking lot. They must be working together again tonight.

"Did you hear me?" Joseph asked.

Nick had not heard anything Joseph had said. "Sorry, I got distracted. Say it again?" Nick apologized while trying to spot the second follower.

"I said, ruin whose life? Stephen's? Why would I do that? Him being arrested ruined everything."

"Ruined everything?" Nick asked.

"Giving the company to him," Joseph replied.

Nick was thrown off for a moment. Regaining his train of thought, he replied, "Giving him the company? Why?"

"It was the only way to keep the family business in the family. Dad knew it. And I came to know it too."

"So you didn't try to ruin him to keep him out of the family?" Nick asked.

"No, I wanted to bring him into the family. I wanted to follow Dad's plan. But just before I announced my plan to retire and leave the company to a successor chosen by my father, I see he's been arrested for defrauding a children's charity."

Nick considered this. While he was, thinking he saw the other man he'd been looking for across the street, watching them talk.

"Joseph, call your driver and get home." Nick had heard all he needed to hear.

"Why?" Joseph asked. He looked at his phone. "It's only twelve thirty. The night is young."

"Because we have company. We're being watched. I caught the same guys arguing with your sister, and an associate of your half brother was murdered not long ago. I can't say for sure what these guys want with you or if they're even after you. But I'd like to not find out the hard way."

At some point during his speech, Joseph had heard enough and called his driver. "My car will be here in about two minutes. Anything else you'd like to ask me?"

Nick thought about it and then asked, "Did your dad have a safe at home?"

"Yeah, in his office, behind the painting of his first factory. Why?"

"Have you opened it?" Nick asked.

"I haven't been able to yet. I don't know the combination. I've been putting it off, to be honest, calling a locksmith. I doubt there's anything of company value in there. It'll likely be sentimental items, and, well, I just am not ready to process that yet."

Nick saw a black SUV pulling up to the curb. "I think that's your car."

The black Mercedes SUV stopped in front of them. The man in the passenger seat got out, opened the door, and held it until Joseph got in. The car took off, merging quickly into traffic, and after a quick left turn, it disappeared due across the bridge into downtown.

Chapter 24

Victor MacArthur, or Mack as he liked to be called, had once applied to be a detective when he was still part of the police force. He was a capable young officer who scored well on the written exam and had top marks in physical fitness and marksmanship. He was passed over for the promotion due to his psychological evaluation. He lacked the ability to think outside the box, which was a necessity for detective work. He displayed a lack of lateral thinking or so he had been told. Still he continued to apply to the detective service and continued to be rejected.

He was, however, well suited for the uniformed service. His lack of lateral thinking served him well as a rank and file uniformed officer. Adherence to protocol and ability to follow orders made him a standout among his peers. His attention to detail and need to stay within the bounds of proscribed doctrine kept him in the good graces of his superiors. And despite being turned down for a detective position, he was promoted to sergeant and made a field training officer.

Mack had been thinking about how, despite his lack of lateral thinking, he had made a decent private detective as a civilian following his dismissal from the police force. Then there was movement. He saw his mark moving down the street, and he followed at a distance, keeping an eye on his target without being seen. Or so he thought. When his target suddenly stopped, it was obvious he was spotted by that damned PI. To make matters worse, he was almost certain he was recognized. Luckily, Mack wasn't alone. After passing by the target, his partner, who'd been following from across the street, should pick up the trail so that Mack could circle the block and stay out of sight of the target but where he could watch his partner.

A year ago, Mack would never have allowed his target out of his sight, spotted or not, partner or not. He just didn't trust anyone to take on such a responsibility, especially when a paycheck was on the line. And this was a big paycheck. In the last few months, however, his partner had really proven himself. Grover Lua, who always went by Lua, applied to work for Mack about two years ago. He had no experience and no qualifications to work security at a private party, but Mack was having trouble filling all his open positions. He preferred to hire current or former police officers, but this party happened to overlap with a major sporting event in the city, and most of the guys he relied on were already working overtime or had already accepted an offer to work the party. Out of desperation, he agreed to give Lua a shot. The kid was definitely green, but he listened well, learned fast, and, as Mack came to find out during the party, could handle himself in a fight.

On a whim, Mack offered Lua a full-time job. Lua took it immediately. It took work and time to train him, but Lua took to it well and became a competent investigator, assisting with many of the cases Mack was hired for, primarily following suspected cheating spouses or finding people who owed someone money. There were some real cases too. In the last few months, Lua had come into his own, handling cases by himself, running security details, and essentially running Mack's business while he was working on this one big case. He was, and still is, hoping that this case would allow him to retire and hand the business to Lua.

Coming out of the alley about two blocks back, he could see Lua. His phone buzzed, a text from Lua, "On the move, headed north."

Mack replied, "I see you. Cross over and meet me at Twenty-Third Street. We'll follow from there."

Mack had felt odd about this last job. It was hopefully the conclusion to a larger and more complex case than he'd ever worked, and it had required some less than legal work, but the reward was significant and worth the risk. Still, he didn't like the idea of going after another detective. He especially didn't like having to take out Santa Claus. Mack didn't really believe in Santa Claus and definitely didn't believe this detective, Nick Saint, was the jolly Christmas elf. Still, lots of people believed it, and from what he could tell, Nick Saint had done a lot of good for the community. And this was why he brought along Lua. Should he hesitate to bring harm to this guy, Lua would not. Lua had a degree of mental flexibility that allowed him to justify his actions even when they may not be justified. It could be an inconvenient trait if not controlled and put to good use.

Lua and Mack met at Twenty-Third Street. They followed Nick for another few blocks to Twenty-Seventh Street. The plan had been to follow Nick to either his car or somewhere they could force him into an alley. There he would be given the option to drop his case or be permanently taken off it. Lua patted the gun on his hip, just to be sure it was still there. They continued following Nick for several more blocks—Twenty-Seventh to Thirty-Seventh to Forty-Second Street. The bar scene had cleared out around Thirty-Fifth, and around Fortieth Street, the area shifted to retail which was, by and large, closed at this time of night. The streets weren't deserted but were mostly empty with residents headed home and those who had to park far away looking for their cars. By Fiftieth Street, they had crossed into a light industrial area, and the streets were empty.

Unexpectedly, Nick took off in a run. Lua and Mack gave chase but were quite astonished by the speed of the older man they had been following. Mack was the first to fall behind. Panting and with a stitch in his side, he wheezed, "Keep…going… I'll…catch up…"

Lua continued but slowed at Fifty-Fifth Street, having sprinted at full speed for five full blocks.

Nick didn't seem phased and continued for another block, then turned sharply to the right and into an alley. Less than a minute later, Lua made the same turn and was struck by a strong pine-scented wind. A few moments later, Mack caught up, out of breath. "Where'd… he…go?" Mack asked as he gasped for air, his lungs burning.

Lua pulled a small flashlight from his pocket. The alley was short, maybe thirty or forty feet long. There were no doors or windows in the alley. No trash cans. No dumpsters. And no Nick. "He should be right here," Lua said, shining his light around but seeing nothing.

Mack backed into the street. "Are you sure it was this alley?" Mack asked as he backtracked, checking the previous alley while Lua went ahead on one alley. No sign of Nick.

They met back where Lua was sure Nick had disappeared. They both looked up when they heard the *click, click, click* of footsteps on metal. Lua shined his light up. "There!" Lua exclaimed.

"Where?" Mack asked, looking around.

"There! Up on the rooftop!"

Mack looked up and saw, running just outside the beam of the light, a dark figure that Mack thought looked like someone wearing a fur coat and hat.

They looked for twenty or thirty minutes but could not find a door, a ladder, a fire escape, or anything Nick could've used to get up on the roof. Lua even tried climbing the wall but couldn't. Defeated and without any sign of Nick on the rooftops, they walked back to their car. Both agreed it was the most ill at ease they'd ever felt.

"It's like we're being followed," Lua said, "but when I look, nobody is there."

Chapter 25

Nick had assumed once Joseph was in his car, that Mack and his yet-to-be-identified associate would disappear. Nick had assumed they were there for Joseph. He had already had a hunch that Joseph was not the mastermind behind Stephen's troubles. He had heard enough to know that coordinating and executing a complex plan was just not in Joseph's wheelhouse, and he didn't really seem to benefit from the fall of his half brother as no one even knew who Stephen was. The timing was curious too. If Joseph was to be believed, he didn't find out about his brother until sometime after his father's death, but the setup had to have started shortly after Michael Jr.'s death. There simply wasn't enough time to put it all together that quickly. Whoever did this knew about Stephen for a while.

Nick had been considering all this as he watched Joseph's car turn and cross the bridge before disappearing into town. When he looked into the reflection on the shop window again, his tail was still there. He hadn't moved. Nick started walking north, away from his car. As he started walking, he saw his tail moving too, and he was sending a text. Nick continued walking, seemingly unconcerned, as though he didn't notice he was being followed. Around Twenty-Fourth Street, he spotted Mack, now walking with his partner. They walked side by side in lockstep, always a block back from Nick. He led them out of the busy strip, through the retail district, and out into the deserted industrial district. Uncertain of what they could want from him, Nick could guess as to why they wanted him. Likely he'd been asking the right questions of the right people. Not wanting to find out what they wanted as they were as likely to try and kill him as they were to try and scare him off, Nick broke into a sprint when he was confident they were in an empty part of town.

Like a leaf before the hurricane flew, Nick was off at a terrific pace. Over the nearly whistling wind that rushed past his ears, Nick could hear the quickening footfalls of his pursuers. These quickly became softer as the distance between them grew. Shortly, Nick was aware that only one set of footfalls could be heard. It was then he made his move. He turned into the next alley and was soon upon the rooftops. He could've easily sat down and stayed hidden at this point but felt there could be some value in being spotted before disappearing from sight. He never underestimated the psychological impact of seeing something that could not be explained. Simply disappear and they would assume he'd found a way out and find him again and pursue him again. See him do something seemingly impossible? Well, they may pursue him again, sure, and they may not, but they'd definitely be more cautious when they next encounter Nick Saint.

Nick followed the pair, moving from rooftop to rooftop, quietly and unseen. They walked back the way they had come, pausing occasionally to scan the rooftops, looking for Nick. They passed where Nick had met up with Joseph, and they passed by Nick's car. They stopped about a block past Nick's car and got into theirs, an older model blue sedan. It had the look of a retired police cruiser, especially when you considered its driver, but Nick recognized it as having previously been a rental car, likely Watts or some other national rental chain that off-loaded its older sedans for new ones. The giveaway was the hubcaps. Police cruisers didn't have hubcaps but rental cars did, a cheap but quite shiny faux chrome set that gave their cars some shine. Three of the four hubcaps were still on Mack's car.

At first, Nick had been pleasantly warm while watching them from the rooftop. They made a few calls; Nick could tell because he saw the screens of their phones light up their faces before bathing the sides of their heads in light and then suddenly going dark as they put the phones up to their ears. An hour later, Nick was cooling off, wishing he'd worn a warmer coat. He hoped they would leave soon. He'd been much colder before, but city living had softened him over the years, and he was no longer used to or in love with the bitter cold as he once had been.

It was two thirty in the morning when Nick saw exhaust escaping from the tailpipe of Mack's car, the engine turning over for the first time in hours in the cold. Nick had lost sight of Mack and his friend an hour ago as the windows fogged over. A few minutes later, the defroster had cleared the windshield, and Mack pulled out into the thinning traffic. The bar crowds, having been expelled at closing time, were just now leaving for home or wherever they were off to next.

In a flash, Nick was on the ground again and moving quickly toward his car. His sudden arrival on the sidewalk took a bachelorette party by surprise. They shrieked and laughed, wondering where this older man had come from and how they didn't notice him until just now. He darted across the road and into his car, the engine rumbling to life.

Nick was off and tailing Mack, having caught up to him a few traffic lights later. With the thinning traffic and Nick's less-than-inconspicuous car, one would think Nick would be spotted quickly. However, Nick had a way of not being noticed if and when he wanted to remain unseen. And tonight, he wished to remain so. Mack crossed a bridge into uptown, passed through the college campus, which was mostly deserted as winter break had come. They passed out of campus and into the older monied part of town where the streets were empty and the houses dark.

Mack pulled into the driveway of a large stone home, passing through the open entry gate leading to the wraparound driveway. There was a burst of light as the front door opened and a figure stepped out onto the porch.

Nick couldn't make out a face from across the street, the backlight of the door silhouetting the figure. As Mack parked, Nick noticed that he parked next to a familiar vehicle, a black BMW. "Ho, ho, ho! Very interesting!" Nick laughed, and he took off into the night, having seen all he had needed to see.

Chapter 26

After the events of the last few days, Nick's already disrupted sleep was all but nonexistent. He had finally made it home sometime after three in the morning and had spent the next few hours tossing and turning in his bed, hoping that some sleep would give him the space and clarity he needed to put together the few remaining pieces of this mystery. When sleep would not come, he lay awake in bed, staring at his ceiling, the light of dawn creeping in and gently illuminating his room.

Something had been bothering him about his conversation with Joseph Honor last night. Nick believed him when he said that he had been prepared to give the family company and a share of the fortune to his half brother. Still, Nick could tell that Joseph was holding something back—a big something. His heart was burdened with guilt, and Nick could feel it. Unfortunately, they had been interrupted by uninvited guests, leaving Nick with no time to try and get Joseph to unburden himself, something Nick felt Joseph desperately wanted to do. He turned their conversation over in his mind. Nick finally landed on it. "He said he beat them. He beat the board when they were trying to sell the company while his father was ill. But how? He had about as much influence over the board as I would have as long as his father—"

Nick sprang from his bed, now certain of what was the matter. He dressed quickly and was out the door in a flash. The streets were empty at this time on a Sunday. The predawn quiet of the neighborhood was broken by the rumble of a V8 coming to life on a cold December morning. Nick's car, a 1937 Lincoln-Zephyr, always started no matter the weather though it would still cough and sputter until the engine was fully warmed. Nick loved his car, having had it painted a cherry red, trimmed with gold, and a custom reindeer hood ornament made it his own. No one had ever seen Nick wash it, but no matter the weather, his car always shined as bright and clean as the day it rolled off the lot. Many enthusiasts were surprised that there was a scratch, dent, or spot of rust to be found despite it being used as a daily driver. The cream-colored leather interior bore no signs of wear or cracking either. "I just take good care of my things," Nick would say, often with a wink and nod.

Nick pulled into the parking lot of St. John the Baptist just after seven in the morning. The vast empty lot would soon be full as the first service of the day started in just a little over an hour. Catholic churches, Nick had noticed, tended to have pretty full congregations in general, but as Christmas approached, they would fill to capacity. Like fair weather fans who only come out to cheer for their team when they are winning, there seemed to be a significant number of holiday faithful who came to worship only when it was a major feast of the year. Not that Nick was surprised, it had been that way for as long as he could remember.

Cars began to arrive, in twos and threes at first, then the trickle became a steady stream. Nick was soon unable to see the full sweep of the lot and had yet to spot the man he had come to see. He stepped from the warmth of his car, not bothering to shut it down, as he figured on being back inside soon enough. He walked in the crisp cold air toward the entrance, hoping to catch his mark before he made his way inside. It didn't take long before he saw Joseph's driver exiting a minivan with wife and four children in tow. They were all dressed in their Sunday best and walking briskly toward the building.

The children, upon seeing Nick, began to giggle and wave, something children often did. Nick did his best not to scowl and politely waved back. As the family entered the building, Nick spoke, "Excuse me, sir? Could we speak for just a moment?"

"It's not really a great time for a conversation. I'm about to be late for church, and, well, as you can see, my wife and I have our hands full."

He turned to continue into the building when Nick said, "I can make it worth your while. Christmas is coming soon."

The children turned to their father, tugging at his coat. "Daddy, please go speak with him! He'll bring us presents, you know he will!"

Their father, unsure what to say about this but not wanting to make any more of a scene, turned to Nick. "I'll be right back, Mr.?"

"Saint, Nick Saint."

The children squealed with delight at hearing the name, and their laughter echoed through the otherwise quiet and somber building. After calming them down and finding a pew for the family, Joseph's driver returned.

"I recognize you," the man said. "You were with Mr. Honor last night."

"I recognize you too. You drive his car," Nick replied.

"I'm one of his drivers, that's true. What can I do for you, Mr. Saint?"

"I'm a private investigator, looking into a case involving Mr. Honor's brother." Nick saw confusion on the driver's face.

"Mr. Honor has a sister. You mean his sister, correct? Ms. Honor?"

"No, I mean his, until recently, long-lost half brother."

"Well, I can't be much help there, Mr. Saint. I'm just a driver, and I didn't know about this brother until just now. So unless you want to know what type of tires are on the Mercedes or the gas mileage of the Land Rover, I'm afraid I just won't be of much use."

"Let's just start with a few simple questions then. What is your name? And how long have you been driving for Joseph?" Nick asked.

"I'm Christopher. I've been Mr. Honor's driver for almost five years. The hours can be hard with a family. Still, it pays better than driving a taxi ever did."

Nick said, "Pleasure to meet you, Christopher. You have your hands full with a big family like that. Do you like your job besides the pay?"

Christopher thought for a moment. "I guess so. Like I said, the hours are tough with a family, and Mr. Honor can be demanding."

Nick asked, "Have you ever felt uncomfortable at your job? Have you had to remain quiet about things you didn't approve of?"

Christopher considered this for a moment. "I guess so. I do have the confessional though, so I'm able to get things off my chest even when my contract forbids me from otherwise disclosing any information about Mr. Honor."

Nick paused, listening to the organ music beginning inside. "You have a nondisclosure contract then? You're not to speak about your work with Mr. Honor?"

"That's correct, Mr. Saint. So as I said, there's not much I can help you with," Christopher said. He, too, had heard the organ begin to play and wanted to join his family.

"What if you knew or suspected a crime was committed? Would you still feel bound to honor your contract? Or would you want to do the right thing?"

Christopher stopped, his brow furrowed, and he pulled Nick in close. "Who did you say you are working for?"

Nick looked Christopher in the eyes. "What happened on the day Joseph's father died, Christopher? You remember that day, don't you?"

The color drained from Christopher's face. His body became tense, and he looked around as though he were afraid. "Nothing happened that day." Christopher turned to leave, a look of fear on his face.

"Christopher, I can assure you, no one is listening to us. And I have no intention of getting you into trouble with your boss. I just need to know what you saw that day. Your name will never be a part of it."

Christopher turned back and, in a half whisper, asked, "Why do my kids think you'll bring them presents? Why do they think they know you? Have you been following us? Asking my kids questions? Who are you?"

Nick looked Christopher in the eye. "Just tell me what happened that day, and you'll have answers."

Christopher started back into the church as the choir began to sing the opening hymn. He stopped at the door, turned around, and walked back to where Nick was waiting. "If I tell you this, you promise I won't be involved in any way?"

"I promise, Christopher," Nick said.

Christopher took a deep breath then began, "Mr. Honor's father had been sick for a while. When he first took ill, Joseph visited nearly every day. He was concerned about his father. He talked to the physicians. We went to the hospital when he had tests. We stayed late into the night. Mr. Honor was deeply concerned about his father. He never said anything to me or any of the other driver's about it, but he never would say anything to us anyway. We're there to go where he wants, when he wants. I could tell though, all the drivers could, he wasn't going out. He was visiting his father a lot. He sometimes cried on the way home. After a few weeks though, he stopped visiting as often. I started taking him downtown to his father's office. It seems with his father incapacitated and unlikely to get better, at least that's what the gossip among the staff was, Joseph decided to move into his father's office and take over. We started going in early and staying late. He was working very hard. We avoided going out to the bars. He didn't take home young women anymore. That is until the day he got into the car very angry. He was cursing and mad. He had us take him out on the town. Man did he go on a bender that day. It was a long night. After that, things started to get out of control. Apparently, Mr. Honor was not as discreet as usual that night. Questions started being asked. For my part, I said nothing. I've got lots of mouths to feed."

"I know most of this already, Christopher. I'm interested in February when Joseph's father died." Nick was trying not to be impatient, but he wasn't interested in the lead-up.

"Mr. Honor visited his father the day he died. I drove him out early that morning. Mr. Honor was pretty distraught on the way over. He was wringing his hands. His eyes were red like he'd been up all night or crying. He was pretty disheveled. Normally, I drop him off at the foyer and then park in the garages. I wait in the staff area until the car is called for. Joseph asked me to keep the engine running. He said he wasn't staying long, which was pretty unusual. Not just keeping the engine running but the short visit. It's a long drive out there. You usually don't just drop in for a minute. Mr. Honor came back about twenty or thirty minutes later. He had tearstains on his cheeks and a bit of a wild look in his eyes. He told me to drive. When I asked where to, and he said anywhere but there. So I took him back to the city and dropped him off at home. When he got out of the car, he left his gloves, an expensive pair by the looks of them. I tried to get them for him, but he told me to get rid of them."

Nick's eyebrows rose at hearing this. "And did you?"

Christopher looked around again. "You sure you don't work for Mr. Honor? You're telling the truth about this half brother?"

Nick smiled. "Trust me, I'm not here about the gloves."

Christopher stuck his hands in his pockets and pulled out a very expensive pair of black leather gloves. "I told my wife they were a gift, but my priest knows what I've done. I did my penance."

Nick laughed. "I'm sure you did. How long after that did you hear about the passing of Joseph's father?"

"I heard about it the next morning. Mr. Honor gave me the rest of the day off after I left him off. I drive him most places, but he does have a car of his own. It's not unusual to get sent home when he's done for the day, even if it's early."

The sounds of the initial hymn had died down, and the call and response of the Mass had begun. "You'd better get in there. You'll miss Mass, Christopher."

"That's it? You're not going to answer my questions? I thought we had a deal?"

Nick had already turned and started to walk back to his car. A stiff, heavily pine-scented breeze blew into his face and swirled around Christopher, who was starting after Nick. He stopped to touch his inner jacket pocket. Something was there that hadn't been before. He pulled from his pocket a rolled piece of paper tied neatly with a red ribbon. He opened it with trembling hands. It simply read:

> Christopher,
>   You should consider finding alternate employment. As a thank-you for speaking with me today, please stop by the law offices of Thomas and Yves. They have an opportunity available for you should you be interested. As for your children, tell them I'll do my best to deliver.
>   Sincerely,
>   Saint, Nick

Christopher looked up from the letter, his mouth open slightly. "How'd you...," his voice trailed off. Nick was gone and so were the gloves.

Chapter 27

It was December fifth. It was Wednesday. Nick liked Wednesdays. Today, he read his three papers leisurely from the chair behind his office desk. He drank hot coffee and ate spiced ginger loaf he picked up from the bakery down the street. Since the events of Saturday night, Nick had been busy, and tonight he would be busy again. But this morning, he had nothing left to do but relax and enjoy his favorite day of the week.

Nick had finished up *The Times* and was absentmindedly spinning his pipe between his fingers when the intercom on his desk buzzed. He pushed the button to talk. "Nick? Let me in, will ya?" It was Rudy. Nick looked at his watch. It was just past eleven thirty. Nick buzzed open the door.

Rudy came in and sat down, having hung his coat over the back of the chair. Nick offered a slice of gingerbread, which Rudy declined. "None for me, thanks. Everybody is bringing baked goods to the office. It's only the fifth, and I'm already sick of Christmas cookies."

Nick smiled. "I can only imagine what too many Christmas cookies is like."

Rudy smiled sheepishly. "I suppose you've eaten your fair share too." They both laughed. "So why did you want to see me?" Rudy asked, certain that it had to do with the *Stephen Dash* case, but he didn't want to be presumptuous.

"Thanks for coming, Rudy. It's about the *Stephen Dash* case."

"Go on," Rudy said.

"There's been a break in the case, and well…it's pretty unbelievable. Normally, I'd close the case and hand you the story but…" Nick hesitated.

"But what?" Rudy asked.

"I need you to be ready to publish the story tonight."

"We don't have an evening edition, Nick," Rudy said. "And even if we did, what story do you want me to publish? What's happening?"

"Get your recorder ready," Nick said.

Rudy pulled out his phone and opened the voice recorder app. Once it was set, he nodded to Nick to begin. Then Nick started to tell the events of the last month in great detail. At the end of the story, Rudy sat silently for a few minutes. Then he spoke, "Nick, this is an incredible story, but some of it sounds like pure speculation at this point. I can't run a story like that without confirming certain elements of it. And so far, it doesn't sound like it's completely verifiable."

Rudy was about to say more, but Nick interrupted, "It will be verifiable after tonight."

"So why do you want me to rush the story then? Why can't I wait until tomorrow or Friday and verify the facts?"

"There will be a power vacuum, at least temporarily, at Gabriel Industries. If we wait to drop the story, the board will seize control from the rightful heir, Stephen Dash, and sell the company off. They'll do whatever it takes to get the ball rolling and cut him out of the company."

Rudy thought about this for another minute. "So rapidly and publicly exposing everything and everyone…"

Nick finished the thought, "Buys us time, puts doubt as to the legitimacy of any moves the board makes. Hell, the SEC may get involved and stop any sale until the whole mess can be sorted out."

Rudy thought some more. "If I do this for you…"

"Name your price," Nick said.

"My daughter wants this toy that's just impossible to find."

Nick scowled. "Have her shout the name of it up the chimney."

Rudy smiled. "Thank you, Saint Nick."

*****

After a quick lunch, Nick headed to see Stephen and Holly. He arrived at their home, and this time, his visit was not unexpected. They greeted him at the door, having heard his car pull into the driveway.

"Nick, how are you? Come in," Holly said, motioning for Nick to enter.

He stepped into the foyer. Stephen asked, "May I take your coat?"

Nick kept his coat, saying, "I won't be long." They proceeded to the living room. Nick remained standing and asked, "I need to know for certain you understand the plan, that you understand what you're agreeing to." Stephen and Holly nodded. "I need to hear you say it," Nick said.

"We understand that once you do whatever it is you're going to do, we are going to become instant public figures, and there will be no guarantees it will work." Stephen continued, "My life is already a wreck, and I'm a minor public menace. What more can go wrong?"

Holly looked at Stephen with a wide-eyed astonishment. "Stephen, they've already killed Morgan. What more can go wrong? You could be killed!"

Nick looked at Stephen. "It's true, but I think it's unlikely, if I'm right, that is."

"And if you're wrong?" Stephen asked.

"Then I've played my hand, your secret about your father is out, and you may have a target on your back."

"Oh," Stephen said. "I guess I hadn't fully considered that." He paused then continued, "It still changes nothing. I'm in."

"Good. I'll be in touch. It could be very late or very early, depending upon how things go." Nick turned to leave.

Stephen asked, "I got a call from someone claiming to be my attorney. It's not anyone I know. Do you know what that's all about?"

"If all goes according to plan, you'll need a good attorney. That firm, Thomas and Yves, they come highly recommended. I'll be in touch."

Chapter 28

The sun sank quickly behind the hills. For a few minutes, the western sky glowed yellow and orange underneath the growing canopy of clouds. The air was crisp and cold. Then the brilliant sunset winked out as the sun disappeared completely below the horizon and night fell.

Nick had watched the setting sun as he drove north out of the city. He drove out past the suburbs and the exurbs. He drove past the millionaires' mansions clustered together around golf courses. He drove out to where the housing thinned into fields and forests and farms. As the night grew darker, about an hour from the city, he crested a hill and stopped. In the distance, in the valley below, he could see the lights of the Honor Family estate. He could follow the long rambling drive to the main house, a twenty-five-thousand-square-foot stone mansion. He could see the conservatory attached to the home by a covered walkway. The pool and pool house were close by though closed for the season. In the fading light, he could see the tennis court and, in the distance, a lake. After taking in the view, Nick proceeded into the valley and to the estate.

Nick was passing through the house, having opened the safe in Michael Jr.'s office. It was behind the painting as Joseph had described. Nick hadn't bothered to close the safe or to be really discrete in his movement around the home so far. A place this big had a few servants on hand at all times. Not a bustling hive of activity but a few extra footfalls around the house shouldn't be noticed.

He was moving toward the walkway leading to the conservatory where he had entered the Honor family home and where he had planned his exit. He had a document from the safe tucked under his arm. He stopped in the living room. A fire had been lit since he had last passed through. Sensing he wasn't alone anymore, Nick turned as the lights came on, a grand chandelier filling the room with light. His eyes narrowed as he tried to adjust to the sudden brightness. He could hear the sound of a pistol being drawn from its holster.

"Hello, Mr. Saint," a female voice said.

"Hello, Ms. Honor," Nick said. As his eyes adjusted to the light, he looked at the older man with the scar on his left cheek, his pistol drawn but held down at his side, the muzzle pointed at the floor, for now. "Mr. MacArthur, I presume? Or shall I call you Mack?"

Before Mack could answer, Nick continued, "Which would mean those footsteps I hear coming up behind me could only be Mr. Lua." Nick turned to find the younger man who had followed him the other night. His pistol was also drawn, but unlike Mack's, his was pointed directly at Nick.

The two men remained silent. Sarah spoke, "You're trespassing, Mr. Saint."

Nick cut her off before she could say anything more, "Technically, I'd say I'm burgling." He held up the document in his hand. "What do you think, Mack? You're the cop." Mack started to speak, but Nick cut him off again, "Sorry, ex-cop. I forgot."

Both Sarah and Mack looked uncomfortable. They had expected to surprise Nick and lead the conversation, but Nick had almost seemed to expect them. Worse, he had taken over the interaction and was throwing off their plan.

"I'm sorry I interrupted you. How rude of me. Do go on, Ms. Honor."

Sarah was momentarily taken aback. It felt like being on stage when someone missed their line. You know what comes next, but the pacing is off, and it doesn't feel right. Luckily, having been through that experience, she was able to quickly recover. "You're holding something of mine, and I'd like it back."

Nick had circled slowly, the fireplace now to his right, and Lua had moved to face him, the fireplace to his left. Sarah and Mack had moved too, standing to face Nick as well. Mack was just to Nick's left, Lua just to his right, and Sarah was standing directly in front of him. "Do you mean this?" Nick asked, holding the document out in front of him.

"You know that's what I mean," Sarah replied, reaching for the papers.

Nick pulled them back from her grasp. "Now if I give you these, what will keep you from just getting rid of me? What leverage do I have?"

"Leverage?" Mack asked. "What leverage? I could shoot you right now and just take the damn thing."

"True, but I doubt you want to. Another body would be very inconvenient. And in the Honor family home, no less?"

"We could clean it up. I know you work alone, so who would know you're here?" Mack asked.

Sarah looked concerned and said, "We're not killing anyone, Mack. Not yet. Just give me the papers, and you can walk out of here."

Nick handed the papers to Sarah. She took one look at the front sheet, then tossed it into the fire. Nick watched them catch fire, the ink causing a blue-green flame to spread across the page. "Before I walk out of here, I'm curious if I got the story right."

"What story?" Sarah asked.

"The case I'm working, Stephen Dash, your brother. I wonder if I got it right."

"Half brother," Sarah said.

"You should walk away while you can," Mack added.

Nick, noting Lua's gun still trained on him, replied, "I'm not so sure you're going to let me walk out of here at all. Otherwise, that gun would be lowered." Nick glanced at the fireplace, the papers now fully engulfed in flame, the top sheet just black carbon curling up and exposing the sheet below as it burned to nothing.

He continued, "See, I had thought Joseph was at the heart of this whole thing. He seemed to have the most to gain. He was the heir apparent to the company, that is until Stephen Dash came into the picture. Once your father decided to hand the company over to his bastard son and cut him in on the family fortune, Joseph would no longer be the heir. He would have ample reason to take him out of the picture. And, at first glance, it seemed to fit. Your father gets sick right after he tells Stephen he wants to bring him into the family and the business. Joseph assumes control unofficially. Your father dies, and Joseph officially takes control. Then a few months later, his only rival for the company is arrested for embezzling money from a children's charity."

Sarah interrupted, "You too? His only rival? It's like I don't exist! First, my father, then my brother. Now you? All my life, I've been on the periphery, always in the shadow of Joseph. Sure, Dad loved me, but he didn't see me as anything but a little girl my entire life. I was pushed into the arts and other 'feminine' pursuits."

Nick interrupted, "But you have an MBA, don't you? You run a fairly successful theater?" Sarah nodded. "I'll get back to that," Nick said. "I was hired to find Morgan Wood, Stephen's supposed accomplice in the embezzlement scheme. He was just a pawn though, collateral damage, if you will. Stephen couldn't have been the primary suspect in the case because he didn't have the hands on access to the money that the accountant, Morgan Wood, did. And the accountant couldn't hide shadow accounts from the board without the treasurer's help. So whoever set up Stephen needed to set up Morgan Wood as well. They just didn't count on three things. First, Wood would have an uncorrupted hard drive with data prior to the injection of falsified data. Second, that Wood would recognize something was wrong and run. And third, that he'd figure out who set him up and how. When I took the case, all someone had to do was follow me to Wood and solve the problem."

Nick turned from Sarah to Mack. "But you were only supposed to take his laptop, not kill him. Sure, you got the laptop after you shot him, but that opened another investigation. If Wood was alive, he could talk about setup all day long. Without the evidence on the laptop, he would've just been ignored. The evidence on the Little Drummer Boy servers was against him. Dead though? Well, now someone was going to look into that. Someone was going to look for his killer. Did you know he left a copy of the laptop for me to find?"

Nick turned to look at Sarah again. "I can tell by your face you didn't. It doesn't matter though. It's just a copy of some files on a thumb drive. No judge would take that into evidence. It did lead me to Faith Garza though, but you already knew that."

Sarah shifted uncomfortably. This was not going at all how she had planned.

"And Faith, not by her choice, led me to Albert Zane, the new corporate counsel for Gabriel Industries. Seems he knows Faith and you." Nick turned to look at Mack. Then he looked into the fireplace again. The papers were almost completely burned.

Mack spoke, "Is there a point to any of this?"

"Sarah almost had me convinced she had no involvement, except she sent you after me, after I caught her yelling at you in the parking lot. See, I had thought you were accosting her, and she played into that. But when I saw you following me, I knew you were the same guy from the parking lot and you weren't some disgruntled actor. I'd had a chance by then to look into you a little more. You were one of Zane's clients. No doubt about it. So I thought about that night in the parking lot. Sarah was yelling at you, not the other way round. I'm guessing she was unhappy about the murder?"

Nick looked to Lua. "And I'm guessing you pulled the trigger, considering you're holding the murder weapon, but Mack took responsibility with the boss."

Mack shifted uneasily. Mack looked at Sarah, but she was fixed on Nick. Mack looked at Lua. He looked scared. His pistol was still pointed at Nick, but his finger was still off the trigger.

The papers in the fire gave off one last wisp of smoke and then were nothing but carbon. Nick grinned. "I fear I may be wearing out my welcome here, so I think I should wrap this up. Sarah, your father loved you but never felt like a woman, especially not his daughter, belonged in a boardroom. A notion that Ms. Dawson tried to convince you was bullshit. Women are equal, if not superior to men, in the pursuit of business. She convinced you to get your MBA. I noticed a few years ago the Honor Family Cookies Presents came off your advertisements. You couldn't convince Daddy you were a real businesswoman when your theater survived on his money. But it continued to survive, even thrive, after you stopped taking his money. You wanted to show him you could do it. You could do what Joseph couldn't. But dear old Dad gave you something else, a copy of those papers you just burned, papers naming your, until then, unknown half brother as his successor. Not only did he give the company to this stranger and not you, but he only did it because he felt the company could only go to a male heir. If I'm right, I bet he even made you witness the document."

Sarah broke in, "And without that last copy you so graciously found for me, this is nothing but a fantasy, a story, like the thumb drive from Wood, inconsequential as far as evidence is concerned."

"We'll get back to that," Nick said. "So you did what you had to do. You signed the papers, and then you called your mentor, June Dawson. The two of you hatched a plan. Take out Dad and frame Stephen, or at least put into place the necessary pieces needed to frame him. Then sell off the company. With her shares and yours, you could start a new business or buy out an existing business. Either way, Sarah Honor would be at the top. But you're not a killer, Sarah. I can tell. These guys certainly"—he nodded at Mack and Lua—"but not you, so you did the next best thing. You made your father sick. I got suspicious when you told me your mom had a conservatory full of morning glories. I passed through there on my way in and was expecting to on my way back out. The Rivea corymbosa is starting to bloom, and it's lovely."

Mack and Lua looked at each other in confusion. "For those of you who don't know, it's also called Christmas vine. Its seeds, when made into tea, produce blurred vision, confusion, hallucinations, stupor, all the signs Michael Honor Jr. exhibited. In an older man, these same symptoms could very well be confused with dementia or Alzheimer's. Too bad his autopsy didn't show any degenerative brain disease."

"Where did you get a copy of his autopsy?" Sarah asked.

Nick ignored the question. "Now we get to the interesting part. Dad gets sick, having never told anyone but Sarah about Stephen, or if he did, it's just another incoherent rambling from an old, demented man. Christmas vine seed, ingested in the right quantities, is actually a psychoactive agent. The lysergic acid amide, or LSA, found in the seeds is the natural equivalent of LSD. Indigenous Mexican shamans have been using it for millennia to get into trance states. I'm just guessing, but I imagine you tried it out as a teenager, right, Sarah? A bored rich kid who has everything she could ever want decides to try out the psychoactive substance in her mom's favorite flowers. It wasn't about the high though. It was about the thrill of being caught. Am I close to right?

"Now where was I? Oh, yes. So Dad is out of the picture. Wheels are turning to take out your half brother if he ever becomes a problem, and your brother, Joseph, is bottled up since he has no real authority until Dad dies, which unfortunately for you and Ms. Dawson, he did. And it's rather unexpected to you since you know he's not actually sick but drugged.

"I think the coroner will agree with my theory that your father was murdered if he looks more closely at that abnormality around the hyoid bone. Someone choked your father, choked the life right out of him. I spoke to Joseph's driver. Your brother was here just before your father died. And he left in a panic. You already knew that though, didn't you, Sarah? Your brother knew the only way to keep the company in the family was if your father died. He did what he thought his father would have wanted. He killed him. It would have been very convenient for Joseph to be taken down for murdering your father. The company would have been yours, and you could've sold it and taken your fortune. When it was ruled death by natural causes by the hospital pathologist, you were afraid to press it further. If the cause of death wasn't obviously a homicide and you pressed the coroner's office to investigate, they might find something you wanted to keep hidden, say the LSA in his blood from a belly full of hallucinogenic tea. So you sat back and waited. You hoped your brother would hang himself. He got caught being a scumbag, again, and you and Ms. Dawson mobilized the board to vote him out on moral grounds. You didn't count on him finding out about your half brother. He came to you, told you about Stephen, just like your father. He told you he was going to give him the company, just like your father did. He didn't even consider you, just like your father."

"Enough! Enough!" Sarah shouted.

"I think you're right. That is just about enough. When Joseph told you about Stephen, you set your plan into motion to take Stephen out. He can't be considered for CEO if he's in jail. But you're never sure what Joseph will do. He's a wild card, right? So Ms. Dawson pulls back from the vote to sell for now. If a major scandal broke, say the CEO passed control to his heretofore unknown half brother who just happens to be caught up in a scheme to defraud a children's charity, well, think of the blow to the share prices. Joseph, fortunately, didn't do anything that dumb. He took a few votes away, but he knows it's only time before he loses them again. The only outstanding problem then was Wood and his laptop. You two"—he motioned to Mack and Lua—"were supposed to find the laptop. Wood was secondary, right? You went to Trails End, same as I did, and what? Posed as cops? I know the actual police never made it there. They really weren't looking that hard for Wood, and I happen to know some people who confirmed that for me. Then when I came snooping around, a good citizen called you thinking you were the police. You came to watch me, to see if I found anything you missed. You were watching me at the lake. You were watching my hotel when Sandy dropped off that envelope for me at the front desk. You followed her and came for Wood when we were to meet. And, well, the rest we already know."

"Great story, Nick," Sarah said. "But like I said, without those papers I burned, there's no evidence. You can't prove anything."

"It's a curious thing," Nick began, "that long ago, people used to ask me for things, toys and trinkets, special treats. Anyone could ask but it was mostly children. In the old days, they used to shout their requests up the chimney to me. Sometimes they would write to me and burn their letters as a way of sending it to me through the smoke."

"What the hell are you talking about?" Lua asked, his finger moving toward the trigger of his pistol.

"He really believes it. You're insane, man," Mack said.

"Believes what?" Sarah asked.

"That he's old Saint Nick, Father Christmas. He's talking about being Santa Claus!"

"I'm not just talking about it," Nick said. A faint jingling of bells was heard as Nick reached a hand out in front of him and, with a flourish of his wrist, grabbed a still warm, steaming stack of papers out of thin air. He turned them over, and Sarah screamed as she recognized the signed copy of her father's will—the one she signed as a witness, the one that left the company to Stephen, and the one remaining copy which she just watched burn in the fireplace.

Mack's and Sarah' eyes stung from a sudden flash of light. Their ears were ringing from the thunderclap that followed. The flames in the fireplace had flared, and cinders were being drawn up the chimney rapidly. Sarah, after her momentary disorientation, became aware of two things: Mack was shouting at Lua and there was a large splintered piece of trim behind where Nick once stood. She could smell that a gun was recently fired. Mack was now holding Lua's pistol and, as her hearing returned, could tell he was yelling at Lua for discharging his weapon. Mack turned, expecting to find the body of Nick on the floor, and realized that he was gone.

"Where'd he go?" Mack shouted, his hearing not yet recovered. He had expected to see a wounded, if not dead, man slumped against the wall.

Sarah shrugged. Then they looked up as the sound of boots running along the roof echoed through the house. They ran to the window, hearing what they thought was the sound of hoofbeats and bells. As they looked out upon the crest of the new fallen snow, they saw the taillights of Nick's cherry red Lincoln-Zephyr as it tore off into the night.

Chapter 29

At about the same time as Nick was tearing out of the Honor Family estate, a breaking news story hit the digital edition of *The Gazette*. The morning print edition followed up with a front-page story of the same though, by that time, most major news outlets—TV, radio, and print—had picked up the story, or at least part of it: "The infamous Dasher of Dreams turns out to be the estranged son of a billionaire and the heir apparent to his fortune and company according to recently discovered documents. His recent legal troubles allegedly part of a plot by as-yet-to-be-named individuals to prevent his inheritance."

Nick walked into the diner and sat down opposite Pete who had his face buried in the paper. "Good morning, Captain," Nick said.

Pete lowered the paper. "It's a hell of a story, Nick. I just hope we can corroborate it. It's easier to get a fair account of things if it's not already adjudicated in the court of popular opinion."

Nick ordered a coffee. "What did the coroner think?" Nick asked, unfazed by Pete's comment.

"He agreed it's fishy, and the pathologist should've been more suspicious about those findings in the neck. We're making a case to exhume the body and get any saved samples from the hospital to the coroner's lab for further analysis."

"And Joseph?" Nick asked.

"He's not talking, but he's been advised to not leave the city without checking with us. He's at home now as far as I know."

"And the others?"

"As you said we would, we picked up Lua and Mack leaving the Honor estate with the missing weapon stashed in the trunk, freshly fired and a bullet curiously found lodged in the wall, near the fireplace."

Nick nodded. "What about Sarah?"

"Same as her brother, silent, but we're looking into her now too. She's also been told not to travel."

Nick sipped his coffee and ordered breakfast.

"Mack and Lua are talking enough though, and they've got lots to say, enough that we picked up Zane for questioning. And Mack is promising us a laptop if we make a deal. He's claiming Lua is the trigger man on Wood, and of course, Lua is spinning it the other way round."

Nick had a look of surprise on his face.

"What?" Pete asked.

"He kept the laptop?" Nick asked.

"Yeah. Turns out he was supposed to destroy it, but he didn't trust his lawyer friend, so he smashed a decoy and kept the real one for an occasion such as this."

Nick let out a low whistle. "I didn't see that coming."

"Speaking of not seeing things coming, why did you push Rudy to release this story early?" Pete asked.

"This story needed to be public. and it needed to be public right away. You said it yourself, the Honor kids are keeping quiet. If I'd just grabbed the evidence and then let nature take its course, well, those kids may never talk. It could be months before anything is conclusive and verifiable. And normally. that's what I'd do: hand you the evidence, tip off Rudy, and let things play out. But by the time anyone got around to exonerating Dash and turning the company over to him, the board would've sold it out from under him. Dash needed this story to come out and to come out right away. The story shed enough light on the situation that I suspect the SEC will step in and halt any sale of the company until it is clear who owns it."

"Smart, Nick. That's really smart."

Nick tucked into a freshly delivered breakfast plate.

"Just one more thing," Pete said. "How'd you get Rudy to do it? He's usually not one to publish without evidence."

Nick smiled. "Rudy's daughter needs a doll that is very hard to find." Nick finished his breakfast and stood to leave.

"Leaving so soon?" Pete asked.

"Yeah," Nick replied. "I've got one last mystery to solve."

Chapter 30

"Fancy a drink, Pete?" Nick asked a surprised Pete Moore.

After the *Dash* case, Pete hadn't expected to see Nick so soon. He definitely didn't expect to see him at the mall, full of shoppers, Santas, and Christmas carols. "How did you even find me here?" Pete asked, looking up from the rack of clothing where he'd been trying to decide what to buy his wife.

As he asked the question, he heard a young Michael Jackson's voice singing, "He knows if you've been bad or good." Pete said, "Oh, that's right, you see me when I'm sleeping and when I'm awake."

Nick pretended not to hear him. "You're looking in the wrong size and color if that is for your wife," Nick said, a smile playing across his lips.

"Shouldn't you be off handing out candy canes and having kids sit on your lap?" Pete laughed as the smile fell from Nick's face.

"About that drink," Nick said, "are you up for it?"

Pete considered it for a moment. "Business or pleasure?" he asked.

"Business," Nick answered. "The last piece of the *Dash* case."

"And that would be?" Pete asked.

"Faith Garza," Nick replied.

"She finally talked?"

"Hardly," Nick said. "But she didn't need to. She already said enough."

Pete thought for a moment. "Can it wait? I'm obviously not great at buying gifts, and I'm running out of time."

"It involves a dirty cop," Nick said. He held up a burgundy sweater. "She'll like this one."

Pete said, "I'll drive."

*****

Nick and Pete sat down at a high top table near the bar. There wasn't much of a crowd at this time of day. Even with the holidays approaching, most weren't out for a drink this early. A waitress stopped by the table and took their order: a beer and a rye neat for Nick and a club soda for Pete.

"Not joining me, Pete?" Nick asked.

"Not if this is business, Nick. You know that."

Nick laughed. "I know, Pete. I still like to ask though."

Pete said, "So I can't help but notice we're at the bar where Faith Garza worked. Are you going to tell me what this is all about?"

Before Nick could answer, the waitress returned. She placed the drinks on the table. "Back again so soon, Kris?" the waitress asked.

"At least you brought a friend this time, a rather handsome one at that." She gave a flirtatious laugh but changed her tone quickly as she noticed Pete rubbing the wedding band on his left hand. "Well, at least you're not alone. You boys call if you need anything else."

"Kris?" Pete asked. "Like Kriss Kringle?"

"Shut up. It was all I could think of in a pinch."

"So what's the deal, Kris?" Pete smiled. "You've obviously been coming here for a while now. What's up?"

Nick took a sip of his whiskey and a draught of beer. "Okay, Pete, here's the story. The first and only time I talked with Faith Garza, she told me that she was forced to go to the Little Drummer Boy, that she had gotten into trouble and told someone her secret, and that instead of helping her, they used it against her. She did what she did to keep out of jail and to be able to see her son. You know her story, found passed out in her wrecked car, drugs under the seat. And you know she was a client of Albert Zane."

"I assume that it was no coincidence?" Pete asked.

"You are correct. I figured once we got Zane, she'd come clean with her story. What power does he have now? Except she didn't come clean. I thought more about her story. She said she told him her secret, and they used it against her. Him and they, Pete, him and they."

"Yeah, so?" Pete asked.

"There was more than one person involved. I had first thought she meant her lawyer. Who else would you go to with your secrets? So I came to where it all started. I came here for a drink. I ended up staying for a while. See the bartender over there?" Nick pointed to a young woman in her late twenties.

"I see her," Pete said.

"She'll be joined by another bartender as the night gets busier. They work in pairs. Faith worked back there," Nick said.

Pete looked at his watch. "Normally, Nick, I don't mind your long-winded exposition, but could we hurry this up a bit? It's my day off, and you're making me work."

"Fine," Nick said. "The bartenders, I noticed, were running a good business back there, not just serving drinks. They're pretty slick, but if you watch long enough without being noticed—"

Pete interjected, "Something you are very good at."

"Something I'm very good at." Nick continued, "If you sit long enough, you'll notice they're selling something besides liquid refreshment."

"So Faith was selling too. We found her stash."

"That's what I thought at first," Nick said. "But I've been here every night for two weeks. Those girls don't take the merchandise home, and, this is important, they never drink on the job. They aren't running the show. The bar owner is, Pete."

"Okay, Nick, you have my attention," Pete said. He looked at his watch then pulled his phone from his pocket and sent a quick text.

"You're wife?" Nick asked with a knowing look.

"Yeah, she's not going to be happy I'm working on my day off."

"Sorry about that," Nick said. "I just needed your complete attention for this one." Nick took another sip of his drink and then began, "Faith was working the bar but wasn't part of the side business, but I doubt she was unaware of it. I think she got worried that the police were onto the side business and were going to take everyone down and that included her. She may not have been dealing, but she didn't stop it. She could be an accessory to the crime if nothing else. What she really didn't want was a third strike and to lose her son, so she confesses what's going on to a cop—the wrong cop. I think the bar had protection from a dirty cop, and she was completely unaware of his connection. So she tells him what she knows, thinking he's the one investigating the bar, not the one protecting it. She has now just confessed her secret to someone she thought would help. The bar owner and the cop running protection then set her up. They slip something into her water, and she loses all memory from there on out. They put her in her car, and someone drove her home with intentional recklessness."

"Intentional recklessness, Nick?" Pete asked.

"Yes, you heard me. If you look at what happened, there's lots of superficial damage and destruction, and it appears all over the place, but it bounces back and forth. One side of the road, then the other, it's not random. And the damage is all superficial. Someone under the influence—"

Pete broke in, "Won't regularly drive from one side to the other of the street to only just graze a parked car or clip a mailbox."

"Right," Nick said. "The driver was deliberate to cause damage but still get the car to Faith's home and park it in her yard. They had to go between two parked cars and miss a mailbox. Too carefully executed if you ask me. And the driver's door was open, but she was found in the passenger seat. After all of that, you tell me that Faith had the wherewithal to put the car in park, open the driver's door, and then climb into the passenger seat to pass out? And why were the drugs under her seat, Pete? That's a terrible place to put them. I'd think they'd be in her purse or somewhere accessible." Nick looked at his watch.

"Got somewhere pressing to be, Nick?" Pete asked.

"Nope. I'm right where I need to be. And almost when I need to be there."

Pete said, "Nick, it's a great story, but there's no real proof. It's just a theory without proof."

"If you want proof," Nick said and pointed to the door.

"Sebastian Henwood?" Pete said, startled to see the narcotics detective walk in. Pete tried to hide his face.

"Don't bother, Pete. He can't see us here," Nick said.

"What do you mean he can't see us, Nick?" Pete asked, as they were seated just a few feet from the bar.

A strong pine scent had entered with the detective. "Just trust me," Nick said.

Pete had known Nick long enough to just go with it. "Okay, so he can't see us. What am I looking for?"

"Just watch," Nick replied.

As they sat and watched, Sebastian Henwood sat at the bar, ordered a drink, and chatted with the bartender. Instead of paying for his drink, however, the bartender slipped him an envelope. Sebastian peeked inside, slid it into his pocket, and left.

"Well, Pete? What do you think?"

Pete looked at Nick for a minute. "Did they just pay off a narcotics detective?" Pete asked.

"They certainly did. And if you want corroboration of the story, you know who to ask. I think he delivered her to Zane, and Zane could get her a good deal if she did the job at the Little Drummer Boy. If she refused, well, she'd be on her own."

Pete didn't hear that last part, however. He was already on his way out the door, hot on the heels of Detective Henwood.

Epilogue

Christmas morning

It was a white Christmas, the kind you think only exists in movies. A heavy snow fell throughout the night. In the morning, the streets were blanketed in white. The world was a quiet place as the sun rose. Nick knocked the snow from his boots and hung up his old worn red traveling coat, the one with the fur lining. He sat down in his favorite chair, put his feet in front of a roaring fire, and sipped hot coffee. He'd had a busy night.

*****

Stephen and Holly awoke feeling the best they had in months. Just days ago, the courts dismissed Stephen's case, given the overwhelming evidence to support the theory he had not embezzled any money and instead was the victim of a plot to keep him from his inheritance. Their accounts had been unfrozen, and it looked like Stephen would soon be the next Gabriel Industries CEO and heir to the Honor family fortune.

When Stephen and Holly went downstairs for breakfast, they were shocked to see all their furniture and belongings were in the house. A note tied with a red ribbon sat under the Christmas tree. Stephen unfolded the letter and laughed as he read out loud. It was a bill from Nick for his work on the case. "Even Santa needs to eat, I guess," he said, marveling at his home.

*****

Faith Garza's present had come a few days earlier. After his arrest, Detective Henwood confirmed what Nick had suspected: Faith Garza did not drive herself home that night. Faith's charges were dropped, and her son was returned home. Waking to the sound of his excited voice on Christmas morning was something she would never forget.

*****

Sandy Anderson had been home for a week, still stiff and sore from the accident but feeling better than she had in the last few weeks. She was surprised to see a large envelope under the tree. She nearly collapsed when she found the deed to her uncle's property. There was a note with it, suggesting she donate the camp property to a newly formed nonprofit started in honor of Morgan Wood.

*****

Glen's wife woke to find opera tickets in her stocking. She thought it was cute of her husband to sign them, "From: Saint, Nick."

Lucy woke to find she had Internet access and a subscription to all her favorite streaming services.

Rudy's daughter found the doll that was impossible to find from her "Uncle Nick."

And Billy woke to find the ball he'd asked for underneath the tree with a note that said, "From: Santa—check the fireplace." And there, by the faux electric fireplace, were two sooty boot prints and a half-eaten plate of Honor Family cookies.

About the Author

Jonathan Morris is longtime lover of storytelling. He started telling his own stories at a young age and never stopped.